THE IKON MAKER

a novel by

DESMOND HOGAN

Writers and Readers Publishing Cooperative

Writers and Readers Publishing Cooperative (Society
Ltd.) 9-19 Rupert Street London W1V 7FS England.

First published in 1976 by The Irish Writers'
Co-operative, Dublin 2, Ireland.
Reprinted 1977.

This edition published by Writers and Readers
Publishing Cooperative 1979.

Printed in Great Britain by offset lithography by
Billing & Sons Ltd, Guildford, London and Worcester

To R. R. Zanker

The men in the forest they ask it of me
How many strawberries grow in the salt sea?
I answer them back with a tear in my eye
How many ships sail in the forest?

Song

1

When Spring came she looked westward. Down the sliding road, over the hills, to where Galway city lay. The Spanish Arch, Claddagh buildings, the lovely, the decayed, horses, tinkers and memories of her husband George as a young man fresh from a peat jungle.

He worked as a builder's labourer in Galway before the war. Making houses where now doctors lived. Then Galway was a place of mystery— cobblestone, Spanish faces, gipsy eyes. The ceaseless roar of waves and ladies, in black, crouching about the Claddagh. Ladies, dark and moronic. Pipe-smoking women.

Their eyes like arches. Holding no fear and always their trek about Galway marked by Gaelic conversation.

Not all of them wore black; there were those in scarlet with blue and green patterns.

After the Spanish Civil War Susan always associated them with Spain, these women in scarlet.

Their eyes were always blue— glass-blue— they seemed to snare some of the sea. There was one called Maire who had hair like eels and watched the sea as though for Spanish ships.

Everybody in Galway then seemed to be waiting for something; the sun in these last years of the thirties crumbled on old stone. Vegetables hung in the air like infants. Galway was an exciting place and she and her husband-to-be took a ride on an old red bus to Barna.

By the sea.

They'd watch sea-gulls— white— and virgins.

For everybody then was a virgin.

Girls in sandals or girls in bare feet walking the tide.

Girls walking on a shore.

The laughter returned now.

9

Voices hidden, sea-weed sprawled like names.

Autographed silences; yes, it had been lovely come evening in Barna then. The sun swallowed in holes; orange devouring every shape, penetrating the wind-shield of a car.

An old Ford coupé placed along the shore.

One would have expected Norma Shearer to emerge.

For such were the days then.

You could recognise Joan Crawford in the face of a nun on Salthill.

A bony-faced nun. For the world was full of expectation. Most of all at the markets. Men speaking Irish, vigil of smoke rising from clay pipes. A gangster-movie playing at the Estoria; Dillinger re-incarnated in the face of a draper's assistant.

Yes, there'd been sadness too, wrecked lives, men from Galway and Clare trekking to England, a long silent march. Faces that didn't know how to protest.

People packing up, going towards the streets of Birmingham, Nottingham, London to earn crusts or packets of soup for families tawny, bony like themselves. The march of history.

People reversing their paths. Once they'd gone Connacht-wise. Before Cromwell's soldiers. Now they were going back.

The Midlands flying by, the peculiar sombreness hanging over Midland Ireland.

Cottages, children, the beginnings of the peat industry.

Towards galless ships and the Irish Sea. Susan herself had gone on one of those ships, she and George, before being married in Kilburn, in a church dedicated to the Sacred Heart.

Galway, a few impenetrable hours had floated back.

They'd had to face life in the raw; Irish faces prone with anxiety.

Building a universe in a world where they were unwanted.

Susan had registered her own protest; as her husband worked she'd go to Kew Gardens or Haymarket.

She'd visit antique shops, go to museums, look at portraits of Queen Elizabeth or other henna-haired women of that time.

She'd escaped; she wasn't going to be shoved downwards. She attended concerts in parks though she didn't like the music.

In Hyde Park, cloistered by the sounds of Bach, her mind would wander back to home, a cross-roads there where people once gathered at evening and danced jigs— solemnly— as though waiting for death.

Skirts rising, arms brawny. A druidic stare on the faces of passers-by.

Or a waltz. 'Come by the Hills.' People dancing rhythm-ically, dancing carnivorously; waiting for dark or still-born children.

Waiting for emigration or anxiety.

And once or twice a year a carnival touched on the village, 'The Lakes of Killarney' painted on the caravans. And again as the lights of bulbs died out people would dance to the music of Slievenamban, a melodeon crying like a cat in one's sleep and someone echoing the refrain: 'In the Valley of Slievenamban.'

Funny, it seems like yesterday, Susan thought one day, remembering concerts in Hyde Park when she'd recall her version of home. But yesterdays slip away, she shought. Youth is gone before you'd see a swan drop a feather. And what are you left with?

The memories of bulbs, bright and blue, at a cross-roads in 1939.

2

These days were waiting days. Essentially. She'd buy bread and butter and Mrs Conlon would ask:

'Have you heard from Diarmaid ?

Mrs O'Hallrahan would say 'yes'.

'Of course.'

And she, Susan, would go into awkward explanations as to how Diarmaid was working as a petrol-pump attendant.

11

'Isn't it something,' she'd say, though she didn't really believe it.

Didn't believe petrol-pump attending was anything despite the fact that Diarmaid wasn't working as a petrol-pump attendant.

The fact was she hadn't heard from him for weeks now; the last time was after January.

It had been snowing then and lakes in the fields were frozen and few cars passed her door-step.

She'd wander up to buy groceries then and wonder at the eternal loneliness of life. Here she was a widow with an only son in England. The year was 1972.

It had been over thirty years since she married. Her first child had come late. Riddled with miscarriages it had seemed she'd had no chance of a child until 1953, back in Ireland, here at home, she'd miraculously become pregnant. She grew big like a cow. Her belly had ached and she'd carried a child like a big pod of lazy flesh. She'd been very big. Almost too big. She'd sauntered through the village and made phone calls in a kiosk to Ballinasloe where her husband worked. There one day he informed her he was leaving for the States. He was fed-up. He needed a change. Change had been the wrong word. He was fed-up of Ireland. He needed rest from a country getting on its feet, feeding itself into post-war bureaucracy.

Every day then the papers bore images of Irish leaders making deals with foreign investors. Ireland was becoming just a little better off; cars ran to Galway for Sundays.

Ballinasloe had new houses. The village, though, still had its poverty and its tedium of Guinness signs and young men with holes in their trousers.

No, this village still was given over to alcohol. There had to be something else.

'I'll make a lot of money,' her husband had said. 'I'll make a fortune.'

'We can live happier then.'

He'd left her and she still pregnant. No, it wasn't his fault.

He loved life, needed it.

He'd been to the war.

Inside he was scarred; he'd met with Russian soldiers, American soldiers, he'd been in the British army. He'd seen Danzig after the war, been to Belsen. He needed life. He knew what it was all about. There was no time for rest, life was motion; he'd known burnt out cities in Europe after the war and he'd drunk gin with American soldiers who'd entered Berlin. Yes, his head still rang; he'd known the blisters of bombs in the sky, planes. He'd seen buildings gutted and dead soldiers affirm their shapes on soil.

He knew what it was all about. Funny, in 1954 when Diarmaid was born he was dead.

He'd died in an elevator accident in Chicago, an out-of-work salesman. 'George,' she'd cried. His body was brought back. It was draped in the Irish flag; apparently he'd once joined Sinn Fein.

Went to meetings in Galway with Constance Markievicz's picture on the wall, listened to men speak in Irish of the GPO burning on Easter Monday, 1916.

Little impressed he'd left it. But they remembered it and draped his coffin. He was buried beside a well in a grave-yard.

She was sure the baby inside her would die, but he was delivered on Easter Monday, 1954. A boy. Safe. In Portiuncula Hospital, Ballinasloe, and in memory of an Irish fruit vendor in Haymarket she called him Diarmaid.

Mrs Conlon cackled now. 'Tell him I was asking for him.'

'I will to be sure.'

'Something good will come his way.'

'I'm sure it will.' Mrs O'Hallrahan moved outwards. Yes, it was Spring all right.

Sheep trod along the road; alongside them calves swayed. And lambs. Somebody's animals gone astray. Then a farm-hand appeared.

She walked nobly through the village.

In the school voices shouted their sums; a statue of the Blessed Virgin Mary stood outside it in glass. Her nose was

13

chipped and her feet which held a snake were decayed.

Roses were made of plastic; their lives over, too. Ugly. Like golf-balls. But Mrs O'Hallrahan praised Mary. She prayed often now, Susan did.

Prayed that God would deliver her child from harm.

3

A letter arrived from him— unexpectedly. Brown the envelope was, colour of his flesh.

She tore it open. His hand-writing was unchanged from the time he was sixteen. Large, dangling, the "a's." Like puppets.

'Mama,

   I'm coming home,' it read.

And more.

'Maybe I've been too long here.'

She was overjoyed. She sauntered up to the grocery shop.

'Diarmaid's coming home.'

'Great. When ?'

'Next week.' Though he'd never said.

'That's wonderful.'

Mrs Conlon wiped her brow. 'I'm sweating.'

A stray dog entered the shop, a big, shaggy fellow.

'What will he do then ?'

'Maybe go to college. Maybe I'll afford it next year.'

'That would be marvellous. He could do agricultural science or something.'

'Certainly. He needs a break.'

She left the shop, Susan did.

Outside a certain blueness had amassed over the fields, colours smouldered, giant shadows ran.

She was happy. She went up the road a mile and a half to tell her mother.

Her mother was eighty and lived in a cottage with Susan's niece.

The niece was quite on in years too.

Susan had married in her teens, so had her older sister, Jennifer, who'd been born when her mother was seventeen, which meant Jennifer's oldest was quite old herself now. Middle-aged. Jennifer had died of lung cancer and her daughter, Alice, looked after the octogenarian. Peeled carrots for her, fed her though she was able and loved the sunlight, walking laneways where lambs dazed past, sunlit.

'Mammy, Diarmaid's coming home.'

'He's not gone long.'

'Long enough.'

Alice stood in a corner. Her face always seemed rigid. Like a goal-post.

'Will he stay long ?'

That was a good question. Susan suddenly realized maybe he wouldn't wait, maybe he'd tire of home.

There was nothing here for him.

'I hope he will,' she said simply.

Alice produced a chicken.

She was a sad lady but a good cook. Long ago in Dublin a half-caste sailor had jilted her and since then she'd lived in shadow.

Here in this kitchen. Sometimes she went to dances with teen-age girls and who knows but sometimes she lay in the fair-green in Ballinasloe for young men.

She had a bad reputation, Alice had.

Susan wouldn't have known but she sometimes heard people talk under her window at night.

Wild words from young men.

She looked at Alice almost bitterly now and realised that Alice knew what life was all about. People like her always did.

4

He was to return on 20th February. This she found out in a further letter.

That morning was very pale— lace curtains blew, colours lay stranded in the fields. A hen whistled— its voice shot through her, and distantly a train shot by, loudly wailing. It was faraway, the train, a monster in her imagination. It used bear Diarmaid to Ballinasloe once to school; after he'd ceased at National school. He used go to school, clumsy, awkward, cold, a succession of jumpers on him, red and blue, and eventually gold.

And his hair dangled, penetrated by light. But as such he'd changed. His hair had grown longer; his face lost some of its pallor. The last time she'd seen him, towards the close of summer, even that had changed. He'd lost the turnip shape, the high forehead; he'd walk in the fields in August, collecting mushrooms.

When he was three he'd done likewise.

'This one has a face like a clown,' he once said to her, picking out a huge, elephantine mushroom.

Long ago; he was four or five.

And last summer he'd gone back to the fields, walking where Jacobean soldiers once fled before the Williamites. After the Battle of Aughrim.

Last summer Diarmaid had collected pails of mushrooms; when it rained he didn't fail to walk the fields. When it was fine he was still there, a scattering of poppies in the garden when he returned.

And she'd have her programmes of Irish music on.

'Danny Boy.' Songs she didn't want to hear anyway, but such words surrounded him.

He was fated. She knew that.

Something about Diarmaid frightened her; his eternal silence. Like a bus-load of autistic children she'd once seen in Dublin. On a wet day. He was so tied up within himself. Like a shoe all knotted up.

Diarmaid was like something that had long ago silenced itself; a cry.

Making dresses she reared him; she opened a little clothes shop, lilac-coloured frocks, linen dresses with roses sewn on.

Gaiety had somewhat taken over the village, people wore her dresses, loved them, except those who were too snobbish to buy them and went perpetually to Cassidy's in Dublin.

She made first communion frocks for little girls, outfits for young boys. A successful dress-maker, she'd arrange flowers in her window.

People would pass, look in, wave. And she'd be sewing under a picture of the Sacred Heart.

With time she changed that picture. She put instead a reproduction bought in Dublin.

A little boy writing, bent silently over a desk. On the back she saw that it was painted by a French painter and the boy was the painter's son.

Diarmaid was her son.

He was ten when she realized what that meant; she'd fed her life into him.

She'd watched him, fed him, she tended to him with a sense of dedication.

And watched him grow in a harsh environment of loss, of alcoholic farmers, of stone walls.

Diarmaid was a dreamer. As a child he looked after kittens, called them 'Pussy'. He bought a budgie in Galway one day. When the budgie flew away he'd cried for a week. Then an uncle bought him a hamster, his grandmother bought him a rabbit, another uncle presented him with a lamb and he tended his flock like a junior Christ, watching his rabbit nibble lettuce and his hamster scoop about a cardboard castle. he'd designed.

But the animals disappeared— just as the circus that came to Ballinasloe every year disappeared— and what was left was Diarmaid's stunning sense of identity. He made shapes, put bits of cardboard together, egg-shells, fluff— mattress fluff, ducks' feathers. He constructed these ikons, was proud of them, brought them to National school, where the old teacher praised his efforts as he praised a little girl's bunch of premature marigolds.

'Daft,' she once heard a woman say of him.

'That child should have his head examined.'

Susan was hurt, angered; yet she welcomed this rebuke. She could withstand failure. Her husband George was a failure. Her whole family were failures. She could construct something from that.

She could make something of it. All her people were emigrants.

They'd landed in Britain. A brother in 1955 committed suicide by jumping from a bank in Kilburn.

Bald, small; he'd lost out. They found him broken like a frog on the pavement. They buried him in London.

It wasn't right to bring him back her mother said. Let him be, let his spirit be.

Now Diarmaid, too, threatened failure, something over-preponderant about his forehead. Something over-exact. She raised him quietly— little was said. His jumpers knitted politely against the texture of the fields. His eyes almond-coloured.

At night they'd listen to Irish comedians on the radio. And one night, Friday night, when he was nine, President Kennedy's death was announced and Diarmaid wept.

He wailed.

Tears soaked his cheeks.

And the next morning she found he'd wet his bed.

Then he went to school in Ballinasloe, Saint Ignatius' college, some miles outside town. Took a train from Woodlawn each morning, weaned on cold weather, winter fog, going to learn maths, geography, history, wandering off there with some other boys who seldom spoke either.

The years, thirteen, fourteen; difficult years. Quiet years, sombre years. Diarmaid did his sums at night, painted little pictures.

Read books which didn't interest him; a new kitten he'd had had grown up and he often softened by the fire with it, stroking its fur, black and white.

She'd make tea for him; they'd eat scones, floured with freshness. They'd listen to Country and Western music on the radio— 'My Wild Irish Rose'— feel safe with one another. 'Are you lonesome tonight?' Mrs O'Hallrahan's mind would seek some image in London immediately prior to the war, a café, toasting beans in a coffee-shop. A woman's veins sticking out like rhubarb.

Nothing would pass between herself and her son. They'd say good night, sleep maybe, as thunder passed over, or sleet, and in the morning, cabbages frozen, Diarmaid would trek off to the station at Woodlawn, to attend school in Ballinasloe.

Sometimes she worried lest he tired of this procedure. He wasn't very good at school; his marks were just about average. He was good maybe at biology and sometimes he scored high marks in art. But that was all. She wanted to do better for him, seek a better position for him.

She wished she had enough money to place him as a boarder at school. Then— almost by God's volition— she won the Sweep. That's what people said though it was only five hundred pounds she got.

But enough at the end of a dark and endless summer to send Diarmaid to school, a boarder.

A local man drove him there. Saint Ignatius' statue looked forbidding, a jackdaw stood on his shoulders.

Ladies left their children there; all talking. Nobody spoke to her, Mrs O'Hallrahan. Nobody knew her.

Diarmaid took a last look at her before he disappeared and somehow she knew she'd betrayed him.

Her business did well that autumn; it flourished. More people were wearing neater, happier clothes.

She was busy. Yet she was lonely and in the evenings went for a drink. A thing she'd never done before. She'd sit and listen to people talk about neighbours' wives.

Apparently there were fewer virgins in the district, more adulteries. And television too, it had its effect.

People said nothing while 'Ironside' a programme about an American cripple, was on. Talk only began during the news. They spoke of Mrs Broderick who was seeing a young dental student in Ballinasloe, or Mrs Kelly who was seen at night with Mr Chapman, an English gentleman come to live in a big house where he played a piano in summer on the front lawn.

And when the late news would start up— and images emerge of war, war in Vietnam, the Middle East, North of Ireland— she could only feel shame.

Somehow she knew she'd left Diarmaid to perish; a loner by nature, he could only become more alone in the nights at school.

But over the year as she visited him she saw him moving towards another boy, Derek. A little fellow from Leitrim, older than Diarmaid, moon-faced. Freckles lay on his forehead like fish. He was Diarmaid's friend, a companion at art class. Together they knocked about. Hands in their pockets, journeys before them through the woods— they made off from teasing boys.

Susan usually found Diarmaid beside a stuffed pheasant; bread hung in the air, holy communion wafers, stale loaves of lunch-time.

Diarmaid was shy of her. His face held a skeleton of displeasure— he was totally enamoured of Derek.

Twice, she'd watch them shy away from her, the two of them off before she left, her bag empty, having brought Cadbury's chocolates and glucose for her baby.

This morning, February the second, she marched past the mirror, preparing for Ballinasloe, the train there.

Her bust was large and healthy.

It reminded her of bucketfuls of something. Chaotic patterns on her dress, urinal shapes.

White on black. Her hair was loud and black; a tiny bit of grey fluff there. Ear-rings. Silver.

Her husband's presents. They'd been on her for years. Ever since she'd seen a bomb drop on Leicester Square. 1942. She'd been walking alone away from a coffee-shop where she'd been watching a Cockney who looked like Adolf Hitler. The bomb dropped, flesh screamed, a tree burned like a

20

frantic dancer. People ran, screamed, but she froze. As though into a gesture which accomplished her life. She felt no fear. Her stance was quiet, unchaotic.

Stolid, she watched a woman run with a child's foot in a tiny strapless shoe.

It was an image she wouldn't forget. Silently she watched. Blood marked the top of the foot and she thought of Shirley Temple singing 'The Good Ship Lollipop.'

Paddy McCarthy called at eleven o'clock. He was going to drive her to Ballinasloe.

'Hello.'

Sunlight caught the wind-shield, penetrated it. Blue.

'Nice day.'

'It is.'

They made off. Past a tinker encampment. A woman wandered with a child and to Susan she looked like an apache in a film.

A dog barked morosely at them— bitten.

A horse sauntered.

Susan waved at the tinker woman and Paddy McCarthy looked at her as though she were mad.

'Terrible goings-on in Belfast.'

'Indeed,' Susan sighed.' 'Its a troubled country.'

'What'll happen next ?'

'Murder, Susan said distantly. 'Murder.' And the word sounded like a Dashiel Hammet story. She said it with the reluctance of a star in a 1940's film.

'That Paisley is a cagey divil,' Paddy said. 'We don't hear much of him these days. He's up to something.'

'No,' Susan said, 'he's not. His day is over. There'll be others now.'

And just as she said it she remembered that the previous evening on television Paisley's image had floated.

A gull careered down. 'Paddy, this country is mad. Murder upon murder. Thirteen dead in Derry, the British Embassy burned down, pub deaths and bombings and that Faulkner fellow. They're selling out.

Rats,' she said simply. 'Rats.'

Later. 'I don't hold a man's politics against him, but when I see the young die that's the end. There can be a million Paisleys and a million Faulkners but can they not realize there's death in store for those that's fallen. The young die. Like hound-dogs. So many die.

They could fill bus-loads with them. Bus-loads.'

And in her mind— frantically— a dream returned. All the dead of Derry and Belfast piled into a bus, skeletons with ties and hats on them. 'I wish they'd all shut up.'

'That Devlin one's a whore,' Paddy McCarthy said.

'A whore.'

'Having a baby.'

'I wouldn't hold that against her.'

And realizing the conversation was getting nowhere she changed the subject— but not before she caught sight of bombing news from the North. A news-sheet outside a shop in Aughrim. It looked old, the news-sheet.

Signs of rain on it. But it bore something of Ireland's tragedy.

Suppressed. All over the land now was an eating sense of grief since the calamity in Derry earlier in the year.

And because gulls hovered over the bodies that day— it had been showing— gulls brought back the television images to Susan. The blitz.

A nun passed them outside Ballinasloe.

She knew nothing of unrest. This was obvious.

Yet Susan felt Ireland's turmoil so strongly now.

All the messages. Ulster Protestants rising, gangs beginning.

They careered down a hill in Ballinasloe.

Past a hospital.

And the North was forgotten. Susan remembered she was about to see her son.

Guns and internment-camps were far away.

The fair-green slouched past.

This was middle-class Ireland after all.

Diarmaid. Her son's name excited her.

She welcomed the idea of him in his anorak.

And was involuntarily reminded of Bernadette Devlin as she looked, a young girl Civil-Rights worker before she became famous.

5

The platform was bare, neglected figures stood there.

Again a nun, her eyes behind spectacles. Beady. Beautiful. She had qualities of her race.

A poster benignly advertised France. Brittany. Mont Saint Michel; shore-line slithering towards a castle.

Susan waited. Fear showed on her face. She didn't know what she was frightened of. Her eyes stared out.

Like someone waiting for news of something.

The train came. No-one emerged at first. Then an old lady. That was all.

Then a young man with glasses.

And a very pre-occupied face. Diarmaid did not turn up. Susan turned away. Fear built up. She wasn't crying. Trembling took over.

She looked back at the station. Silently she cursed the disappearing end of the train.

And then she realized Paddy McCarthy was watching. 'He must have missed the train.'

'Yes,' said Paddy. She entered the car. Quietly a woman passed, head down. She saw the sunlight glare on the tracks.

'I'll come back tomorrow,' she vowed. 'He'll be on to-morrow's train.'

That night she drank Guinness, watched television. Brian Faulkner was being interviewed. Mrs Conlon was knitting a blue jumper for a niece in Australia. Mrs O'Hallrahan got up, walked away. She felt bad had come upon her today because she'd maligned Brian Faulkner. They'd been ill-chosen words.

Cold smote the air; her head reeled, blind spots of red in it as though the aftermath of bomb explosions in Belfast. No,

Brian Faulkner wasn't at fault. We're all at fault, she decided. She shouldn't have spoken ill of him. It had brought her no good.

She made Fry's cocoa for herself. The milk danced. She went to the window and looked out. Peaceably she watched the fields. She prayed Diarmaid would come and inadvertently she saw a tree.

The tree dangled. Yes, it reminded her of a tree in the year Diarmaid spent as a boarder at school. A tree on which his friend Derek had hanged himself. The boy apparently had become preoccupied with the teasings of other boys, one day he walked out to a bare tree in lonesome land and hanged himself. The image stark and amazing, women talking about it. And the boy's figure dancing in everybody's mind. Bred into an East Galway sky on a famine tree. Famine because it was eaten up, the tree, as bodies had been in Ireland once.

Shock, terror had followed. Apparently Diarmaid had never really been teased. He was too quiet for it. He'd just lounge, watching gold fish in the pond. His friend had made an effort of supremacy and therefore suffered.

Suffered terribly. He died on a day the boys ate fish at the school.

Diarmaid hadn't seemed so much shocked as silent after it; he quietened. Again.

Remained inside himself. But it was as though Susan often thought there was a revolver in the drawer of his mind. Something about to emerge. Diarmaid was unsatisfied with authority now.

He was disturbed.

The following year he again attended school as a day-boy. Going from Woodlawn station on March mornings. But now he made additional trips to Ballinasloe. On Saturday afternoons he went and bought records in Salmon's in Ballinasloe. He became part of what Susan had heard so much about. The younger generation. He played loud music.

The Rolling Stones. They were the only names she recalled

because they struck her as downright peculiar.

And she worried a little, Susan did, when she saw Diarmaid's face become just a little like one of the young men's faces on the cover of a Rolling Stones album. It seemed like idolatry going the wrong way. Diarmaid's face sometimes had an almost-girl's look. A cosmetic appearance.

It frightened her. It repelled her. The sounds took up his time— they seemed to estrange him from her— these strangely dressed young men. She almost swore vengeance on them. But there was little she could do. Her attraction was minimal. The attraction of these pop-groups was gross. And when an ape-like face stared from over his bed she felt like tearing it down. The young man in the pop pin-up had over-large lips. Like jelly.

'Pansy,' she felt like saying to him when Diarmaid was at school.

But she realized that was uncharitable. These young people had their ways. And she loved whatever they chose.

Because ultimately they had to be.

There was no reaching them.

They were in a world of their own.

And when Diarmaid left in Autumn he took but one album with him. A Rolling Stones album. The oldest looking of them all. And from that day on she felt a queer affiliation with the Rolling Stones.

They were almost like brothers. Their mouse-like faces; their quivering hamster-nostrils. She felt love for them. They were part of her son's design.

He'd gone to the trouble of buying their albums in Ballinasloe on foggy afternoons.

Her love went with him now and often— alone— she'd probe the left-over Rolling Stone albums as though love itself was about to fall out of them.

But all that came was dust.

The tree tonight now emerged, receded, its horror gone.

'Poor mite,' she thought, remembering past the Rolling Stones to Derek.

'Poor child. Sure as people said of him he was probably not all there.

Too much by himself. It's bad for you.' Inadvertently she realized her own solitude.

She went to bed, crossed herself with water.

Images of the North returned, blood, gore, bodies; she took fright. Her body sweated; she felt her sweat merge with the sheets.

'Jesus. Jesus.' She slept. Soundly. And all the green afternoons returned, Galway long ago with her husband, George. Cabbages buoyed up like circus clowns. Performers, Life was an arena then.

She dreamt she was having her toe removed in a quiet surgery in Galway in 1939.

Then she woke. Faraway a goods-wagon let out a drone. And she felt for Diarmaid's youth and solitude.

The world was tight with problems now.

She'd ring a taxi, go to the station in Ballinasloe. No Paddy McCarthy today. Her night of agony was over.

But it was only five o'clock. She slept on.

And in a dream she saw Diarmaid behold a ladybird.

Blood-red. A blob on his nail.

His face gleamed. She woke. It was still early.

And words of Christ came back to her. But instead of 'The poor you will always have with you' in her mind now they were 'The young you will always have with you.'

6

Next morning a taxi came from Loughrea. It called at her door. Lazily she answered. As though drugged. It didn't matter now. He'd come. She knew that.

Again sun shone. And a tinker encampment was all colours.

Faces danced out— the old, frozen, suffering faces of Ireland.

Each seemed to have a special design. Like an old lady who

was trembling over a child. Her face lit up, all its contours.

Not much conversation passed between them, talk of the weather.

The taxi-man stared ahead.

He praised the local bishop who'd declared talking about night-dresses on television was wrong some years before.

Susan smiled.

She despised the local bishop, hearing that the woman censured by the bishop for speaking about night-dresses on television later had a nervous breakdown.

'He's a very good man,' the taxi-driver said.

Mrs O'Hallrahan said nothing.

Ballinasloe curved inwards, a different route from yesterday. Trees, glinting branches strong as limbs, reaching out, sparkling.

The railway station lurked ahead, red, white. Susan wondered at the sadness of stations. An advertisement for Woodbines dominated her view; she considered partings, stations, the humdrum meaninglessness of them. All building up into death. Just death. A final desperation.

Her thoughts were dark. She was depressed. She could see nothing before her but death and failure. She found herself afraid. Fearful of her own death. The paralysis motions which led up to it.

She wanted to cry out. Her scream — mental— searched the sky. A gull wheeled.

'Diarmaid.'

That was it. Would he arrive ? Her whole life seemed to depend on that fact. Everything. She remembered underground stations in London during the war. Faces.

A Mongolian face she once saw. Strange. Like something from the silent films which still showed in Galway City.

All memory lugged inside her. Fearful. A French woman she once met in London during the war. A girl, 23, who'd fled the Nazis. She'd had a child. Her husband she'd left in Paris. On a back street. They'd got a lift out before the invading Germans.

27

Her husband had escaped from the lorry. He, 25, awfully handsome, wanted to stay and fight. Susan knew he was handsome from the French woman's description. She also knew he wore a red check shirt.

Marguerite, the French girl, held these details like prizes. They were her gains from life. Despite the fact her husband probably lay dead or castrated somewhere.

She emerged from the car, Susan did. Her hat probed the air, a feather on it.

She walked quietly, hesitantly towards the platform. The Dublin train came in.

Merging, devouring the station.

All was bustle for a moment.

Then in an anorak Diarmaid emerged. Silently she perceived him. Like seeing Veronica Lake walk out a door. She ran. His eyes were grimmer, his lashes blonder. Hair sheathed the smoothness of his cheekbones. They embraced.

There are a few immutable moments in life. One for Susan was welcoming her husband back from Germany after the war. In Victoria Station. He was lovely then. Now Diarmaid, without badges, was in her arms. 'Love.'

He vaguely struggled free.

'Hello.' They walked past the taxi, got in. The taxi-man helped them slide in Diarmaid's case. That was the supreme sadness for Susan. It looked like a coffin. She watched her son again, the care of sunlight on his cheekbones. He'd changed. Really changed. His eyes had points of sapphire in them. He was so fair. So young and lovely and fair. And as she watched she realized he'd become more and more like a pop-star. He was not alone any more, Diarmaid wasn't.

He was part of a whole generation of young people, alive to the possibilities of a moment.

Diarmaid was one such young person.

For a moment he was like a stranger. She wanted to catch something, hold it. Like his eyes. They'd changed, too. Yesterday's almond-coloured brown had deceived her. They were at once more solid. Greyer. Grimmer.

He stalked into the car.

People flashed by. An old lady held a suit-case. Susan felt a depth of inarticulation in her never felt before.

A sweet-shop floated by— in it a swan on an advertisement. The road breached in sunlight.

Traffic was high today. The taxi-cab wandered on, stopped outside Mrs O'Hallrahan's dress-making shop. There a pink dress was shot through with light.

She paid the taxi-driver. Walked on in. With her, a son. A goose who was travelling over gardens quacked at her.

'Well, love, you're home.'

He entered. There was joy on his face. He'd explained how he'd missed the train the previous night. She heard a train ruminate in the distance. Over the picture of the Sacred Heart a shadow was cast.

'Diarmaid you look so different.'

He just smiled and said simply 'I don't feel different.'

She took him at his word.

Outside a school-bus ran.

She felt its colour, yellow, and thought how quickly time passed.

She made coffee. He preferred that now. They ate home-made bread. She often, quite expressionlessly, looked out the window.

He talked of Camden Town, a time with a friend from Dublin there. He'd been working in a Jewish bakery. All the cakes, all the bread had gone by. He'd decided eventually to come home he said, looking at an advertisement for 'Butch Cassidy and the Sundance Kid' in Camden Town.

He'd seen it with his mother in Loughrea once; both had enjoyed it immensely, gone for a walk by the lake afterwards.

And his mother had said, 'You've a bit of a tinker in you.' Why she said that he'd never know.

'You mean you've come back to find out?'

'Not exactly.' Diarmaid was silent.

'I've come back to —'

She knew what he was going to say.

'To get away.'

Wasn't everybody saying it these days?

'No. To be alone.'

The remark lingered; soon it was dark. She made brown bread, cake. Also she made coffee, warm, vibrant coffee. They sat and ate the cake which was a coffee cake.

Diarmaid's pullover was purple and red and mauve. There were collars on it. He sat with arms folded, sleeves pulled up. On his arms hairs spread— a richness. She felt as though she were gliding into the past— towards safety.

They were together again. She turned on the radio. The music that issued was a negro's. Singing a dark song.

'Do what you gotta do.'

The music seemed to tangle Diarmaid's muscles. She wanted to cry out. Instead she went to the window. Outside a train— distantly— imparted silence.

She watched it fade, its lights.

And in her now was the sense of one of life's few moments of peace.

Here was her son. She was here, too. She was happy.

7

He behaved strangely, quietly.

Always by himself, brooding.

Emptying little things on the table. He'd begun making ikons again— feathers, beads, paper accumulated.

All sorts of items.

He began making pictures, Diarmaid did. 'Collages,' he called them, though in Mrs O'Hallrahan's mind they would always be ikons. She remembered an article she'd read on ikons in a missionary magazine many years before. Ikons from Russia, faces of the Madonna in blues and greens, and when Diarmaid started with his odds and ends Mrs O'Hallrahan called him in her mind 'The ikon-maker.'

One day— in March— he created Kew Gardens, all colours,

browns, greys of grass, blues of flowers, a mixture of colours for dresses and one solitary hippie amid the throng.

On him a coat of many colours.

And suddenly Susan realized. That was it. Her son had become a hippie.

Vacant his face was. His forehead sometimes like an old man's.

Something keen, something frustrated, something faraway about him.

The realization was a sad one, a lonely one.

It was like reading something on the paper. Diarmaid was faraway from her now; old in his way, wise in his way.

He walked the streets of the village.

Head down. Strangers looked at him— closely.

And Mrs Conlon peered at him. Out her window. She looked like a witch the way she squinted.

All tucked in. And one day while Mrs O'Hallrahan and Mrs Conlon were looking out the window at Diarmaid they mutually observed one another.

The experience was embarrassing. They both turned away — and probably both in some way had realized they were looking at a misfit.

8

One day by consent of both of them they went to Galway. They took a train from Woodlawn. The morning was bright.

A gull sat on a bench and of last year's leaves one of two were left under a bench.

Beside them a woman smoked cigars; a lady with blue hair and a feather in her hat.

Mrs O'Hallrahan quietly informed her son that the lady was wife of a local doctor. Last year she'd tried to commit suicide by drowning herself in a bog-hole.

She was a sad and lonely woman who drank gins and often stayed— openly— in Hayden's Hotel in Ballinasloe with young men.

'You're gossiping', Diarmaid accused her.

'No', Mrs O'Hallrahan said. 'I'm telling a truthful story.'
The train came.

In less than an hour Galway met them, sledge, sea, white
on it, gulls rearing, clouds closing in over ship-masts. At the
station Mrs O'Hallrahan felt a loud whisper of failure in her,
the last weeks, Diarmaid saying little, maybe telling her about
a concert, a film he'd seen.

Once he described a homosexual he knew.

An old man, Greek, who was forever asking Diarmaid to
sleep with him.

'And what did you do?' she asked.

'Nothing.'

Surprised at her own frankness Mrs O'Hallrahan laughed.

'God you're awful.'

And realizing it was the wrong thing she'd said qualified
her statement.

'No, love, you did right.

There are some people it's wrong to pity though because
pity isn't fair.

It tends to destroy.'

Diarmaid had gazed at her. There'd been a ray of sunlight
fixed in the room. His hair quite white. And he'd looked at
her strangely.

As though she weren't his mother at all but a beautiful
stranger.

Sounds of Galway met them; a young tinker boy sang
'Faith of our Fathers' outside Lydon's tea-house. An old
man begged; young executive types rushed everywhere.

First they stopped in O'Gorman's and there they bought
a copy of Sinead Bean de Valera's fairy stories.

'I'll give it to Etty's child,' Susan said.

Etty was a widow-woman who had two children. She
sustained herself by making carpets. Her husband had died in
a car accident.

Like an increasing number of people in the neighbourhood.

Next they visited Kenny's art shop.

From a painting women in scarlet gazed out.

'Lovely,' Mrs O'Hallrahan said, like a very cultured art dealer.

On the Claddagh their hair shook. Swans moved.

Like a thousand ships.

A priest hurried by and as though seized by something Mrs O'Hallrahan lifted her hands.

'It's lovely.'

Her son agreed.

Together they walked. 'I used come here with your father when salmon swarmed under the weir.'

'That must have been a good while ago.' Diarmaid said, innocently enough.

'Not that long ago.'

In Lydon's they had lunch.

And the modernity of the place was unfavourable. As quick as possible they left, up University Road. Young students floated by on bicycles. A girl and a boy on the one bicycle, blue. Flowers already grew; crocuses on the plain outside college, and the ramparts of the university rose.

'Sure you can go there next year. We'll find money.'

However Diarmaid just looked at her. His anger was small but she recognised, Mrs O'Hallrahan did, that he had no intention of going to college. That soon he'd return to England. Even as his father left for the States. Salthill; water surfaced, waves.

Diarmaid threw in a stick, a dog followed it.

And inside her now Mrs O'Hallrahan felt like a graveyard; hope gone.

The few desolate figures of her life wending towards her.

When Diarmaid had gone to the toilet she sat on the beach, wept.

No-one saw.

And looking up Clare shone opposite her, over the bay.

And inside her a young girl seemed to yawn, the girl who'd married George O'Hallrahan. And the same girl who'd had no

33

idea what lay before her in the line of tragedy. A husband dead and a son— like gulls— distant from her.

9

He'd gather cowslips, return with an impending bunch. Like a little girl. Forehead delicate, eyes auburn. China cups choked with cowslips.

And at night together in the kitchen they'd talk.

Diarmaid quietly recalled London, his winter there, old ladies with ulcers abandoned around Charing Cross, a young man on winter evenings playing a viola; sunsets on the Thames and at night Chinese cafes and faces.

Other Irish exiles looking keenly into space. Diarmaid coming and going to films. His winter seemed more like a summer.

'Your life is so rich now,' his mother said.

And in her mind she was wandering again with him in Dublin Zoo, 1959, when he was small and hippopotami browsed out from grottoes, opening mouths into caves.

'Your life is so rich.' And on an Irish Catholic headline she saw that a bishop was dead.

He walked down a laneway one day. She watched from her mother's house.

His hair in little wiggles. Like Marilyn Munro's.

She felt herself praying for him. Yet the dense area of prayer in her seemed a betrayal now.

Sometimes— sometimes she could almost feel there was no God.

Alice said, 'He's a strange lad.' Her niece. Almost as old as herself.

Alice was pouring tomato ketchup on chips.

She'd been talking about the Battle of Aughrim, the battle which the Irish had lost to William of Orange, the battle fought nearby where many thousands of Irish were either slaughtered or had fled in ignominy. The defeat was remembered vividly, reminisced about in ballads, in folk-stories, in the dying legends of a race.

Her mother lay in bed in the kitchen.

Alice tended to her chips.

'Your son is a strange breed,' her mother said. 'A strange breed.

He'll go far.'

'How do you mean ?'

'Travel afar. He's got wander-lust in him. He's a child who intends to travel.'

'Travel leads you nowhere,' Susan said with unexpected bitterness.

'You never went far,' Alice said. Not with any malice.

'London during the second world war was as far as one could go,' Susan said. 'The bitter things of life were there.'

And she realized she'd gone as far as a person could go.

From an Egyptian restaurant in Soho in those years to blazing flesh and the sight of a woman running with a girl's strapless shoe.

Yes, she'd gone as deep into people as was possible; deeper than most.

She turned about. Her son entered. A stranger in the house.

Under a picture of the Sacred Heart his forehead gleamed.

'We were just talking about the Battle of Aughrim,' Alice said.

'Why that ?'

'We're interested.'

Alice was being funny.

'Interested ?'

'Shouldn't everybody be interested in their local history ?'

'I suppose so,' Diarmaid said. 'Drunk boys in London. Guys from Kilconnell vomiting in Kilburn.'

'Don't say you were among them.'

'No. Not yet.'

His mother looked at him, distraught.

'We live in a sad country,' Alice said into the wash-basin.

And in Susan's mind now, prompted by the remark and by

the sound of suds, were visions of gulls.

Gulls over Galway; the Claddagh wrapped in swans.

All the time swans on the Claddagh in the late forties.

'Funny you should say that,' Susan said. 'I remember George, Diarmaid's father, once telling me Ireland was the saddest country on earth because it didn't know its own soul.

What he meant I never knew until recently.'

Alice looked in amazement. Her mother stared approvingly.

'We just don't know how to manage. Don't know what to do, how to act in extreme situations.

Irish people make fools of themselves because they've no beliefs. No real beliefs.'

She stared out the window.

Most of the time now she didn't know what she was saying.

But looking out the window— fields green and turf glimmering— she realized that at least she'd had a beautiful, a lovely youth.

10

Diarmaid took to her philosophical turns of phrase strangely.

Looked at her— half-suspiciously. The way he looked at television. He didn't really like television.

All in all it had to be admitted that Susan's family— if nothing else— were a thinking family.

Over the days Susan and her son grew closer, walked by ragged hedges together, Susan in a pink cardigan.

And it occurred to Susan that she and Diarmaid were like brother and sister rather than mother and son.

Their laughter rang; Diarmaid patted a donkey one day.

And his mother took a photograph of him.

The boy laughed. Together they ran through the fields and sat by a pond.

'There was a pond like this in school,' Diarmaid said. I used to go there with Derek O'Mahony.' His stance flowered.

He grew larger. It was as though he could speak for the

first time about a subject.

'We were great friends.'

'I know.'

'Mammy, I loved that boy, I loved him so much. I hated to see other boys torment him. That's why I stood beside him. So they'd torment me, too. They never did. They sort of respected me.

I'm not sure why.

He was a funny bloke. He'd write poems about swans and then make paper boats of them. A bit mad. Not too mad though.

He loved Keats and Shelley.

And then one day, one day I suppose he hanged himself.'

On the famine tree, Susan said to herself.

God help us. Christ be with us.

They rose. Perished by a religious truth she drew her cardigan about her.

Stiffened. Walked on. Christ had been nowhere to be seen the day Derek O'Mahony had died.

Everywhere people suffered without a God, Susan thought.

Fearing the verdict of all this she gave up thinking.

But later that night by her bed she opened an old missal— unused for years— and found a declaration. 'Susan, 1938, Galway.'

And she thought— fondly— of a tinker child she'd known in Galway in those years, his feet long and spare— like a swan's.

'God bless your youth,' people would say then.

And she realized, deep in her then, that God was spare in his blessings.

But exact.

He proportioned everything evenly.

Life was a sacrifice, a flow, a gregarious mixture of hope, defeat, despair.

And out of despair— as out of a dark room in a country cottage you found a lovely old earthenware jug— so also you found hope.

Going to buy groceries in the morning she noticed how fine the day was.

Passing by, a tinker said 'Hello.'

And turning about she saw her son, Diarmaid, play with a child.

11

She'd tell him about the war at nights, crippledom of electricity, of transport.

'One day on a platform in Hyde Park a woman got up to sing 'The Vale of Avoca.' An Irish woman. A bit mad. But she was wonderful. It's funny what you remember, isn't it?'

Diarmaid nodded agreement. 'The Rolling Stones play there now.'

'Who ?' — and then she remembered the pale faces, some looking rather like clowns, on an old record sleeve.

'Are they still around ?'

'Well I suppose it's an exaggeration to say they play in Hyde Park. But they're still around.'

Cups washed they went to bed; outside lights burned, subserviently.

It was as though they were graciously bowing before a God.

Some presence in the night. Yet the East Galway nights were lonely ones. Full of cows calving, farmers farting, old women dying somewhere of cancer or a loneliness they'd once picked up at a fair.

This indeed was a countryside of betrayal. The dead seemed to linger. Something unspoken in their lives. Only in summer when poppies vagrantly lined the walls and the sound of Chopin came from the local doctor's house where a woman, his wife, frigidly obeyed the laws of summer.

Somewhere now a curlew called.

She was back in a train going North during the war. Up to Durham through lovely countryside to see a boy she'd known in Galway who was dying of T.B.

A blond-headed boy, not unlike Diarmaid now, up through hills where shadows crossed to a town of pipe-lines and factories. Her mind was again in that train; she'd been reading a book.

Mary Lavin. 'Tales from Bective Bridge.' Some item of Irish literature which had emerged at the time.

The boy, her friend from Galway, of whom her husband George was jealous because in ways he was more beautiful than him, died.

They'd never bothered to bring him back to Ireland because of the war. They'd buried him— funnily enough— in London. Brought his body down as bombers wheeled in neighbouring cities and in the newspapers. Buried him beside a grand-uncle in Harrow.

'Requiescat in pace.' The words came back. Fear also. Would Diarmaid die too ? He looked so like that boy she'd known in Galway. Dismissing the thought from her mind Susan feigned interest in a song on the radio. Billie Holliday, a bejewelled voice from yesterday, singing 'Solitude.'

12

His collages were becoming bloodier, all red; one day he smeared lipstick over egg-shells.

'Is this because of the war stories I've been telling you?' she asked.

'No,' he said simply. He was wearing a brown polo-neck jumper. He looked at her. Blond streaked his forehead and she noticed he'd won a few freckles from recent sunshine. Large ones. Like tadpoles.

'Love, I'm sorry,' she said.

He turned away.

'What are you trying to express?' she asked.

'Derek O'Mahony's guts,' he said.

The answer shocked her, and in it she recognised the re-crimination. She'd put him in that school. The year of Derek

O'Mahony's murder. For that was now what it seemed to be. The murder of an innocent unexpiated person.

She moved towards him, withdrew. Anyway, she reckoned there was enough violence on the television screen in the pub across the road to inspire Diarmaid, the violence of Belfast streets or the untold misfortunes of a Belfast child, his face clinging to the grey and the wet of the television screen.

But over dishwashing she was haunted by his last remark. Derek's death was still not just jaunting Diarmaid but fixating his mind, pivoting towards a point where death met life. His mind was full of skeletons. The skeletons of an Ireland mangled, lost, an Ireland where cabbage seed grew in neglected gardens. Derek had been victim; Diarmaid sympathised with him. Sympathised so intensely he'd also become the boy, stood beside, smelt the polish from his shoes. And yet Derek had gone beyond Diarmaid, walked out one day, left the world for a grim alternative.

And all the time people's voices hushed about the image of the boy, left-over, lost. Derek dangling, regretting his misfortune, putting up with it until with one stroke he'd done what a thousand politicians had failed to do. Condemned Ireland, a country of mediocrity, yet a country which if Derek had remembered, Susan thought, had permitted a relationship as fine as his with Diarmaid, two boys in the same colour pullover wandering over the fields, rugby balls flying, their hands in their pockets, alive to a guilt common to all.

Susan's mind was flying over images. She thought and thought. That year of Diarmaid's in school was one of deep enigma. What had happened? She wasn't sure. Something of cherished consequences.

That night, having made a fire, she stroked her hands.

'Diarmaid, do you feel bitter about Derek's death?' she asked.

'Yes,' he replied. 'Very.'

'Why?'

Singularly he said it.

40

'Because he was killed not just by the repression of a whole country. But by the evil of small minds.

I feel like avenging his death some time.'

A train started up, smashed its light distantly.

Diarmaid continued. 'It's funny feeling that, but I know I'll always feel like that.

In a sense hopeless.

Why had Derek to die? Because people teased him? No. Because they told him he was a misfit from the beginning.

That won't do. You can't tell a person they were wrong just because they're being themselves. But it happens all the time. It won't do. It won't do.'

'No,' Susan agreed.

And she felt her name, Susan, personalized. 'No, it won't do,' she repeated to herself.

Gradually though the realization dawned. Diarmaid had in his strange way been in love with Derek.

She dismissed the thought. It was foolish.

But it lingered. Doris Day cried on the radio, another old song revived. 'Secret Love.'

She'd washed Diarmaid's pajamas, was ironing them.

As she finished ironing them— Diarmaid reading an old book of short stories which lay in the house— she held them to her. Smelt their smell.

Somewhere the scent of pubic hair clung like spring to bark. Therein was life's mystery.

'What are you doing?'

'Being— being—.' But she couldn't think of the word. She left down the pajamas.

He'd scored a point. She wasn't able to forward an explanation.

She sat down beside him.

Together, before going to bed, they ate flakes in warm milk.

That done, they retired. To what were deeply secret identities now.

Linen puckered; she was making a dress for the local doctor's wife. The woman who hadn't spoken to them at the
station one day now had ordered a dress, admiring some of
Susan's work.

Daily the dress progressed; now Susan was rounding it off.

Outside the day was singing, happy. Birds took flight and
earlier Susan, at dawn, thought she'd seen a lark swerve
through the air, a happy aspect about it.

Diarmaid entered; he laid some cowslips on the table. They
were entangled. 'Like a boy's genitals,' she thought. Trying
to put the image out of her mind she misplaced a button.

'How are you, loveen?'

He slumped downwards, heavily loaded. He'd gone for a
long, long walk. Now he was tired. She looked at him.

Closely.

'You look a bit like your father today.' he seemed to
ignore that for the moment. Then he looked towards her.

'You . . . ' But he didn't finish the phrase.

'You . . . what?' she wondered.

Maybe he was going to say 'You are obsessed with my
father.' But that wasn't true. She wasn't obsessed with his
father.

She was obsessed with him. Growingly. She'd always loved
him but now she was afraid for him. There seemed so much
within him, so much that had probably happened to him
which would lie unexplained now. His walks, his careful
meanderings through country lanes, all seemed to stroke
backwards towards a time when she caught Diarmaid one day
combing Derek O'Mahony's hair at school.

Diarmaid was haunted. Simple as that. Not by rain or the
gulls which hung over the school but by the fulfilment of
these images, Derek O'Mahony's death.

That night Diarmaid put bits and pieces together, feathers
for a boy's eyebrows, paper skin, a button in each eye.

'You're doing a boy.'

She was tempted to say he looked like Diarmaid but he
didn't really. 'He's a drug-addict,' Diarmaid said solemnly.

'Where is that indicated?'

'His eyes are blue.'

When they were drinking coffee Diarmaid said,

'In London I saw a boy die in a policeman's arms. He was a drug-addict. Heroin addicted. He was about twenty, twenty-two; he had half a moustache. He was crying. I leant my arm towards him. He took it.

A plane was going by overhead.

I'll never forget it. The last thing he said was "Paul". Who Paul was I don't know. He seemed to be crying out for someone.

An ambulance came and took him away. I stayed there for two hours. Then a man with pony tails tried to pick me up. I walked all the way to Camden Town, getting there next morning!

It was awful. She made more coffee. 'The world is full of terrible things.' And she realized that Diarmaid, basically, was lonely because his friend had gone.

With him a certain hope. The boy in his little art-work was the boy in London but also a face far back, Derek O'Mahony's. The cry of a lonesome facade.

Diarmaid went for a walk. A moon browsed.

When he returned his mother was crying.

'Why are you crying?' he asked.

She said 'I don't know. I don't know. I've let you slip from me.'

14

The tears ceased; there was the desperation of moving towards one another. No-one knew why she was crying. She didn't. Something trundled in her brain. A train taking off from Euston during the war. Back to Galway. 1942. A brief home visit when she visited the city and found a dead seal on the beach in Salthill.

'Diarmaid, I'm sorry.' But later she thought she was crying

because in a sense she'd interned Diarmaid in that school. There he'd taken up a hopeless cause. The cause of that boy. And in a sense she was one of the murderers of that boy. She'd misunderstood the situation. She'd let it carry to a desperate end.

And now in grief Diarmaid was gone from her. Over in London God knows what he was up to. He'd gone. Stricken-faced. He was meeting the woes of the world on Piccadilly, submerging himself in them.

Next day they watched a ladybird on the table. It floated away. The stain of red haunted the darkened air. They looked at one another and laughed. It was very fine, the day and they sat outside and ate brown bread and slices of cheese.

'Run over and get some drink to Mrs Conlon,' Susan said. The boy did. She nearly died of shock, the woman. But there on a bench Susan and Diarmaid drank ale, ate cheese. A passing motorist, face covered in dark glasses, stared.

Diarmaid smiled. That evening, her work done, they walked to a stream. Tears had undone something, made their relationship more perfect.

They could look at one another like children now. Gracing a hedge one morning they found a snail. Diarmaid looked at it and for a moment Susan considered. This was what his relationship with Derek O'Mahony had consisted of. Little details.

She was winning a confidence in herself to remark. She was able to see. Gradually picking up the surprise of Diarmaid's encounter with Derek.

At close of day now light flushed, heavily pink, and cows trod by. Some like ballerinas. Just a little clumsy. She watched, Susan did. The spectacle. On the street corner a poster draped the wall now. For Duffy's Circus in Ballinasloe.

'Let's go,' she said to Diarmaid one day.

And they did. On a Saturday afternoon. She wore a dress she'd worn to a cousin's wedding. White. Rims of blue on it. And before they went— in Cullen's— Diarmaid bought a little bonnet for her which she actually wore. The circus progressed.

And for a dim moment while a splendidly young trapeze artist performed his tricks— Susan watched Diarmaid's gaze. It was on the boy. The boy's hairy chest glistened, soaked gold and brown. His hair was more towards brown. He had a winning smile when he finished his acts and his lips were red. Like a poppy. It occurred to Susan— ingenuously— that her son was a homosexual.

And then— proudly— she dismissed the thought. What would he be one of those for? Yet it lingered, the thought, and when a clown paraded about Susan's mind swam with the green of grass and her nostrils exploded with lion's smell. What had she produced? A homosexual. Yes. Diarmaid and Derek had had a love affair. She wasn't shocked by the revelation she'd just disclosed to herself. It was like picking a salacious bit of news out of a magazine. Diarmaid, Derek had done some terrible thing together.

No. Her fancy was slipping. And yet, yet there was a sort of solemn warning about all her thoughts.

She shouldn't question so much. It wasn't right. No-one should.

At home that night she felt like crying again. But something stopped her. One shouldn't weep in the face of disaster. Had she made her son homosexual? She didn't know. Didn't want to know. Diarmaid sat, reading his short stories. She leant over his shoulder.

He was contemplating a drawing of Leo Tolstoy over a story.

'Tolstoy,' she said with surprise.

'He wrote 'War and Peace' didn't he?'

'Yes.'

She remembered abducting a battered copy of it from an Irish nun in Battersea once and reading a page and a quarter of it.

The curiosity flourished. It was like opening a very gossipy magazine, seeking details of a venture one wasn't supposed to know of. Diarmaid was a decidedly strange child. For his own sake she had to find out more.

'Did you have a nice day?'

'Yes.'

He turned. His face glowed. Like a squirrel's.

'We must have a picnic some day,' Susan said.

'That'd be nice,' he reacted.

'Sunday,' she beamed.

'O.K.'

Sunday they collected cold chicken, a cake Susan had made, bread, cheese, hard-boiled eggs, premature Easter-eggs — small ones that children buy to break the Lenten fast their parents have imposed on them— and they made off.

Down the village street. It was so bare, so sparse today one would think a cowboy would come riding up it.

It had that neglected, smelly sense. Like a village you'd see in a Wild-West film.

They made a strange sight. Susan was dressed in a blue and white dress she wore on her return visit to Galway, 1943; her hair and her skin bloomed.

'Fresh as a daisy,' as Mrs Conlon would say. Diarmaid wore a grey jumper.

He'd banded his hair in a string so that he could have been mkstaken for an Apache.

Mrs Conlon could have looked out her window now and deemed both of them misfits.

By the stream they set down the blanket. Arrayed out in blind flashing bits of food. Diarmaid came back from a few moments' itinerary.

'I've found a statue,' he said. Sure enough, covered in trees was the statue of a mediaeval Irish saint, old.

'It's a funny place for it to be,' Diarmaid said.

'I'm sure someone knows of it,' Susan said.

'But why don't they remove it, bring it to the museum or something.'

'People don't like changing what's old and sacred.'

Diarmaid looked at her at this; an inflection disturbed her. It was as though he were going to say something; put forward some disagreement. But, nothing said, he quietly sat down, not unlike an Indian chief— and began eating.

16

A quarter to four.

Susan looked up.

'Have you ever been in love?' she asked.

'No,' he replied. Then he reconsidered.

He seemed to ask himself the point of her question; he dwelt on some problem in his mind.

'Why do you ask?'

'Oh I was just wondering.'

He thought again, suspected again. 'I doubt if I'll ever fall in love,' he said.

He got up, walked away. There was a huge silence now; a sort of diseased embryo about. Above the sun was momentarily squashed out.

'Darling, what's wrong?'

He faced her.

'I don't know. Strange, isn't it? You'd never have dreamt of asking me that last year. You think I had a love affair or something. Well, I hadn't.'

'I didn't.' Tenderly Diarmaid now spoke. 'I know what it's like to love, though.'

And she saw it clearly, days spent at school, Autumn mist veiling the fields, fences closing in on top of cows, shapes sauntering about; the mystery of winter already in the air, winter, a story untold.

'I know you do.'

But she didn't want to ask did he mean Derek.

Instead she concentrated on the butter and recalled an image of Diarmaid long after Derek's funeral, standing, hands in his pockets, against a background of tennis-playing boys in white.

Diarmaid's head was in the air, his whole stance unswerving when she looked up.

There was a sort of gentle grandeur about him. 'I loved Derek O'Mahony,' he said.

The grub nearly fell out of Susan's mouth— she'd just eaten a lump of cheese.

She stared. What was he saying? She felt her ground— tentatively.

'You— you did?'

She looked down. 'I know,' she said. 'Sure I know. You were a great friend of his.'

'I was.'

He rose, smiled, walked by the stream.

'It's knowing things like that that almost makes death seem O.K.'

'Knowing what?'

'That you've loved. And really loved. Derek died. He must have felt awfully, awfully friendless, but somewhere in him he must have known I cared.

Because I really did. I remember we once pledged undying support to one another by the lake.

A football floated. I held his hand.

Being close to him that day really makes life worthwhile. My life. All lives.

I could live on and on.

I couldn't go back on that.

It's like— like picking up the glove of a child that's dead. I'll go on and on knowing that I was cared for, knowing that I loved. If he had to die at least it wasn't in vain. No, I don't mean that. Of course it was in vain. But something clings.

Like lightning. It's as though God spoke from the heart of our relationship. We were--', He finished.

It was as though his flow was getting the better of him. Susan felt a vast excitement.

It was like listening to poetry she decided.

He was so unerring her son was.

Somewhere he'd chosen rightly; he'd taken up a distant cause.

They ate on, peaceably.

And later that night she realized she felt as she had when Spring was just about coming and she was looking down roads thinking of her son.

He sat up in bed; pajamas open, his chest revealed. She sat down on the bed beside him. For a moment she felt like stroking his chest. It was a feeling of overpowering sensuality. One that hadn't overtaken her since her husband used lie in bed— on mornings— when he wasn't working.

The reaction now was one of shame. She withdrew.

Her son mustn't know of her feelings. But then, considering, she was glad of her impulse. She felt newly, profoundly alive. She'd go on— past feeling— towards a new dimension.

This was love, rekindled, newly awakened in her. She loved Diarmaid.

The time had come not for a relationship between mother and son. But for a new relationship. That between friends.

The lampshade inheld a yellow ochre light. Around it a semi-dark floated. Diarmaid sat up in this. Like a mediaeval saint.

And she thought of the truth she'd heard today. The truth stated between them.

That of a person to a person. Diarmaid to Derek, Derek to Diarmaid. And maybe that in turn situated her to Diarmaid. Faraway she heard a cock cry— it was only night, but the cock seemed to crow from Diarmaid's school, an amount of betrayal. The shrill cry from the heart of Ireland. Yet as she reconsidered there was more to it than that.

In the blind heart of betrayal hope stepped out. Like a cock. Proudly.

Such was her relationship with Diarmaid.

As it had never been before; open, blindly open to new ideas, new consequence. They seemed to be going somewhere now.

Like two people down a country lane.

And as she closed her mind off to sleep a gentle old song smote her mind. 'O to be in Dunaree with the sweetheart I once knew.' And with that she slept soundly, briskly till morning when the crowing of cocks was over and sunlight lay, a new tomorrow.

17

'How did you find it after Daddy died.'
He asked her one night.
'Lonesome,' she sighed.
Almost grief-stricken she watched him. 'I had no-one. Then I suppose I had you.'
He was looking at her quite closely.
'It's sad, life is. You must make the most of it.
And I suppose I did,' she continued. 'In my own way. It didn't matter. It stopped mattering. Life goes on.'
'And what if it doesn't?' Diarmaid asked.
'It doesn't for some people.'
'Who for instance?'
'That boy I saw died.'
Susan turned away, defeated, remembering, even as he said it, Alice, her niece.
'Some people stop living I suppose.'
He was obviously haunted by the last remark, took up marmalade, spread it on his bread.
'That's so true,' he said.
And as she watched him she thought of the trapeze artist they'd seen together, swinging.
And in herself she wondered with pride if this wasn't to be the most she'd get from life, her relationship with her son, these weeks.
But on the floor she noticed crumbs going stale; retreated from that thought. One mustn't think like that. It's not good.
It might bring an end to happiness.
Always afraid of conceptions she dug the table with her nails.

Her Sacred Heart picture gazed outwards; no, she didn't want to think.

And she didn't have to, Diarmaid talked about the war in England, asked her what it was like. And she had to think of the bombs and somewhere in her head their grinding grimacing laughter renewed.

A plate left on the table; a song on the radio later, bed.

And later thoughts. But in the morning when she awoke and saw Diarmaid's face she realized thoughts didn't matter. What she had she had.

And buttercups exploded beside an old stone outside. A donkey brayed and she soundlessly moved about her chores.

18

'Derek died because he wasn't important.'

'What sort of talk is that?'

'I think he sort of forged an identity by dying.'

They stuck in her, those words.

Like hot plates.

Tongs.

The subject pursued its yearning; it was her turn to ask.

'I think you were closer to Derek than you were to me.'

'He was my friend.' They were both eating three bars of Cadbury's chocolate.

'But why had he to die if he was your friend? Surely he'd have had you. Surely that would have been enough.'

The questions flowed. The yearning clung. Questions unanswered. Yet there was an unstable atmosphere of reward in the air. It was as if Derek O'Mahony were becoming something of a concentration point; she was assuming his role.

The intricacy increased; down a bog road she sang 'Come Back Paddy Reilley.' He listened.

'You're thinking of Derek O'Mahony,' she said.

It was the most implausible thing that ever passed between them.

He started. Blond hair flowed down. Dashes— today— of green in it.

He took off an anorak.

The day was too hot. 'You're mad' he said.

She agreed. Didn't say so. She was becoming quite crazy. Her dress was blue and it was as though the moment she'd made that remark summer began. Yellow licked the fields. Buttercups.

She felt excited. And with her son she realized that Derek's presence in his life was far beyond just the indelicacy say, of sexual contact.

It was dark. The colour of trains.

Of waiting at stations.

'Derek was a friend of mine.

He's not, though, somebody I think of all the time.

I don't need to.'

The clowns came back at the circus; the trapeze artist. That was her excitement.

Of a new means of contact.

Derek was like a devouring point and in the trapeze artist now she saw all life flow; her new relationship with her son. She felt as she did in Galway before the war when she used take walks with George.

And his name demanded something of her. George. It rang.

With it the green of little silent bits of grass in Galway.

The green of his uniform later on in war.

They sat down.

'Soon it will be Easter. Your birthday.'

No reply. But it didn't matter now.

Her thoughts were faraway— beyond the hills around which held memories of the Battle of Aughrim— to a time out of mind.

Just the moments of love she'd known.

And as this was one she was totally apart, free, sitting, smiling.

A girl in love again.

19

'Freedom's just another word for nothing left to lose.'

A song drummed over the radio.

Later that evening Diarmaid reprimanded her. 'I wish you wouldn't talk of Derek so much.'

'Sorry.'

'Before he died I guess I knew he'd kill himself. We'd fought.

He threw a copy of the 'Dandy' at me. Little boys read it.

And he went off. Like a spoilt brat, I thought at the time. Then the clue came. He hung himself.

The clown in the circus the other day reminded me of him. Big face; long mouth.

Derek was one of life's failures.'

'Aren't we all?' Mrs O'Hallrahan injoined.

Confessional.

'No,' Diarmaid said.

And went to bed.

She was racked by the thought of it.

The thrown-away 'Dandy'. 'God speed my love 'til you are mine again.' The words of a daft song returned. She took sausages out of the fridge and put them back in. It was as though Rip Kirby had come to life— as though a terrible act had seized the house. Derek's death. Afraid now she sat and silently said the Rosary to herself, a train edging through the sorrowful mysteries like a knife.

'Sacred Heart of Jesus I place all my trust in thee.' And then she reconsidered. Maybe I don't believe in God at all. But a whole life-time of belief— and the exaggerated Irish sense of grave-yards— and Mrs Conlon steadied her. 'Of course, dear Jesus, I believe in you. Love my child.'

Touched by the simplicity of her own prayer she remembered Diarmaid in a cradle and left— herself— for bed.

Little innuendoes; a letter from a cousin in America, all became part of a growing concern for Diarmaid's past. And at church one day she noticed Diarmaid, his blond hair, and wondered at his past. It was so different from his country's life-style. So other than it.

The priest raised the host. She wondered at all the times a priest had raised a host at school and how Diarmaid and Derek had looked on, regardless, knowing they shared a secret, an immense secret, a relationship.

She'd never know the ins and outs of that relationship.

She'd never know what actually happened; other than sometimes watching Diarmaid stroke a snail's back and knowing he must have done the same in Derek's company.

But this she did know, whatever separated them now united her with Diarmaid. The merciless on-goingness in Diarmaid.

His father's relentless spirit.

And in a way now— Mass had ended, they were going forth— she realized, more intently than ever, that she was an alternative to Derek, that what was happening now between herself and Diarmaid was the result of a life-time of waiting.

The doctor's wife waited in a car.

Over her face she wore a black mantilla. Like a face in a Spanish painting that hung in Susan's hallway. She awaited her husband.

Mrs Conlon approached. 'Hello'. And then 'I believe you're going to Galway University, Diarmaid.'

He looked at her with fear.

'Who told you?'

Mrs Conlon looked at Susan and Susan turned away.

Yes, she had told Mrs Conlon a lie. Yes, she had tried to cover up. She turned away.

Afterwards— with the memory of Mrs Conlon's fox fur in her mind— she wept.

Diarmaid threw margarine into the toilet.

'No, I'm not going to Galway University. I'm leaving. Tomorrow.'

'Diarmaid.'

They looked at one another. The recognition was total. They embraced.

Swiftly— as though he had done too much— Diarmaid withdrew. But whatever it was was over, Galway University or not.

A picture of an antelope hung over the range. She sat under it.

'What do you think you'll do?'

'Go back to England.'

She took a breath.

'Do you have to?'

'Yes.'

She said nothing. Later she made coffee. Briskly the tap turned. And she recalled a visit to the Zoo in Dublin in 1958 when Diarmaid was four.

It had been a grey day. Late in April.

Lions had growled. And under Nelson's Pillar later a flower-seller in a Dublin accent had said:-

'You've a grand lad, love.'

Now Nelson's Pillar was blown up.

There was a singular pathos about O'Connell Street in Dublin. As though a leg were missing.

Her son drank from a cup on which a bird— blue— was painted.

'You don't have to go.'

'I must.'

She said nothing.

The following night they went to a concert in Loughrea. A girl sang 'Rose Marie, I love you.' A young man played an old Beatle song, 'Can't buy me love.' The curate made a speech in the middle, and towards the end Elvis Presley appeared.

Or at least a local imitation of him.

It was all sad and old and everything represented in it was already half-forgotten. Like a girl who resembled Marilyn Munro. Then after the show— carnations given to the girl whose lips exploded like Marilyn Munro's— they, Susan,

Diarmaid had coffee in a cafe smelling of haddock.

The street outside was sad and lonely.

Lights blinking on it.

'It would make you cry.' Susan recalled her husband's expression.

A cinema sign said 'Live for Life.' All energy gone they got a bus home. There they spoke again.

They were precious, the moments now. She didn't know when he'd leave, hoped it wouldn't be soon. They'd have his eighteenth birthday together.

So gently she grabbed them.

The feel of things. She watched him. Closely. On Saturdays she walked with him. The Spring was exceptional. Primroses blazed.

Her face— in the mirror— became as a girl's. And in Diarmaid's eyes was the image of the trapeze artist they'd seen at the circus.

His male body gleaming in a white outfit.

An image of love.

Hastening to forget everything she planned nothing.

Then one night watching Diarmaid she became frightened.

He was sitting on his bed, brooding.

'What's wrong?'

'I don't know.'

His face had a harrowed look.

He was crying. 'Love.' 'No.'

His shirt was off.

'What's wrong?'

'Nothing. Go away.'

This she did. She knew something of his relationship with Derek was returning. It had to be that.

In her room she consoled herself.

It would pass, this fright.

In the morning he left for Ballinasloe on a bicycle.

'You can't cycle that distance,' she told him.

'I can,' he replied.

And did. Visited his old school the tree on which Derek

hanged himself, the sheep-flowing fields, visited them as though visiting an old song or turning old photographs. This she gathered that evening.

He went to bed.

In the morning he went out. She found an empty Smartie packet by his bed.

She was making blue shawls for local members of the Legion of Mary.

It was hard not to think but she managed not to too much. He was quiet that evening. A bad sign. He ate nothing.

She watched him.

Then left him. Went to watch 'Ironside' on the television in Mrs Conlon's. A thing she never did.

Mrs Conlon called her aside. 'You look worried, dear.'

When she said nothing Mrs Conlon asked.

'Is it your son?'

She said nothing.

Then Mrs Conlon said, 'But you looked so happy recently. Like a pair in love.'

At this— sobbing in the quiet of her stomach— Susan left.

Hardly bidding goodnight.

At home she wept.

Skyscrapers seemed to crash in her. She wept for being so fool-hardy. For thinking herself young and beautiful and a friend to Diarmaid rather than a mother.

That night she dreamt of porpoises.

In the morning an alarm clock shrilled on another empty day.

22

Good Friday.

At three o'clock a service was spoken in the church. The priest's voice droned. Afterwards people kissed a crucifix, women in black scarves, women in fur coats.

And all remembered their dead and the graves of East

Galway, limestone headstones, names written into the weather. She stood on the gravel, Susan did. No son beside her.

He was gone. Into the fields. She didn't resent his lack of religion.

Somewhere she considered he was lucky to have such intensity, to love signs for Chinese cafes in London. That indeed was religion enough.

They ate brown bread that evening. The jam was strawberry jam.

The silences between them were growing deeper.

Her only hope now was that he'd stay till after his birthday.

23

Easter Sunday; the day was fine and bells sounded.

Clouds like dove-tails rested in the sky. There was a lot of blue; people marched to Mass and their footsteps were quiet, hesitant all the same. Mrs O'Hallrahan looked out. Ready. Here eyes were swollen. She was crying. Last night Diarmaid had said, 'Fuck off,' to her. 'You bitch.' That over an Easter egg he'd broken on the carpet for which she'd mildly reprimanded him.

He didn't go to Mass. Alone she listened to the story of Mary by the sepulchre. The Gardener a Christ.

And she returned home to find Diarmaid had made the lunch. A start at reconciliation.

Parsley sprinkled on the roast lamb; they devoured the meat. The potatoes were roasted.

Stark, yellow with a crust of brown and a froth of white.

They talked little, looked across the table. Outside a yellow car passed with a load of young people. Possibly from Dublin. Umbrellas, top-hats sticking up; all gay and shouting.

Diarmaid went to the window. He was going anyway to the sink with dishes. But he gave a look of such wistfulness outside that she could have cried.

Daily now she'd noticed his urge for departure.

A train sounded. Distantly. A bitter Easter Sunday train.

She went for a walk in the afternoon. Alone. Neighbours passed; an old man with a walking stick. He tipped his hat. To him she was a widow, and a widow was an act of God in Ireland, a sacred profession. She was a singular person in this area. That night over Easter egg wrapping (always she bought Easter eggs at Easter) Diarmaid announced he was going out on a date. She could have died with shock.

'What. '

'I'm going on a date.'

He put on a shirt bought in London. It had green lapels. Altogether when he was finished— his trousers were blue— he looked like an angel.

Her reaction was a mixture of joy and frenzy.

She felt like a clown.

'Who are you dating, may I ask?'

'Sheila Cummerton.'

A girl from Loughrea, it transpired, whom he'd met in a supermarket— of all places— in Ballinasloe.

'She's an engineer,' he told her.

'No she's an engineering student in Galway.'

Jesus. Profanities mounted in her. She felt as though she were reading a comic.

They said goodbye. He slipped away. The boy was in love.

24

They went to a fair in Kiltormer together. This she gathered the following day. Danced in the open air on a warm Easter Sunday night.

'The band was terrible,' Diarmaid informed her.

But that didn't seem to quench his newly-acquired thirst for living. They left again for another dance that night.

This time she met her.

She had olive-coloured hair.

Her whole form stung with fragrance; some delicate perfume.

She had rabbit-coloured skin.

She was nice, yes, but somewhere Susan felt her way uneasily.

'Do you like Galway?'

'Yes.'

And after a minute. 'I like it, but people are stupid there. They drink too much. I like the fellas, but they're sort of buffoons.

I like going for walks there.'

This remark— poetic as it was— helped Diarmaid's point of view.

They were having tea— the girl's spoon slipped.

'I never knew this part of the country. It's new to me.'

'Really?'

'Yes.'

Silence.

After some seconds.

'Where did you get your dress?'

'In Basle.'

'Where?'

'In Switzerland. I was there last summer.'

'How lovely.'

Remarks piled up.

The dress was indeed— memorable. White.

They parted. The two young people slipped away. It was night and walking in a lane later Susan spoke to a sheep.

25

He wept bitterly. She didn't know why Wept for days. His eyes became like liquorices.

'What's wrong?'

He didn't tell. It had obviously broken between him and the girl. These dances in forests of coloured lights in the country beside old crosses and ruined monasteries.

'Love, what's wrong?'

The word brought reaction but no reply.

She'd obviously hurt him. Just as Susan had hurt herself by attaching herself to a youth who happened to be her son.

For a whole week it was like a series of Holy Thursdays. All she could feel were his tears. Then apparently they met again. Were briefly reconciled. Went to a film in Loughrea.

Afterwards to a dance. In Ballinasloe. In the Emerald Ballroom.

But this time it ended for sure. Just as Derek O'Mahony had hanged himself— betrayed by all, even himself— so Diarmaid now launched out against history.

Casually he packed up.

'Aren't you staying home for your birthday?'

'No.'

A mortal wound had happened.

Something irreparable had happened.

Susan's imagination didn't hold itself back. It was something to do with sex. Wasn't everything? and in the same moment she realized— undauntedly— that Derek O'Mahony had finally killed himself because Diarmaid wouldn't have sex with him.

She was convinced now. No proof was needed.

Like herself Diarmaid was pure.

Derek O'Mahony had wanted to consummate their outcast state. Diarmaid wouldn't go along with him.

It might have been pure conjecture.

But like a fortune-teller she knew the truth of her conjecture. Likewise Diarmaid didn't know how to handle sex with this olive-haired girl from Loughrea.

So bitterly it had ended. She could almost see the scene. They were probably playing a gross number somewhere. 'It's a lesson too late for the learning.'

In it all was indeed a lesson too late for the learning. That love always loses. No matter how real it is.

People have no time for love. It's a fool's game.

In his room a mirror reflected his image.

She felt like crying out. Like smashing the image, smashing the mirror.

With forty pounds he went back to England.

Curlews cried in the bog next to Ballinasloe station.

A taxi-man looked harnassed— no work maybe.

The kissed— slenderly.

The train left.

She walked away.

26

The nineteenth of April, Wednesday, passed; no birthday cake. The image she'd entertained, Diarmaid blowing out eighteen candles, failed to realize itself.

A birthday card to an address in London where he might be staying— his aunt's— that was all. A present of ten pounds. She went to see her mother that day, went to see Alice, looked out the kitchen window towards a cow.

And felt suddenly the hunger of the land she lived in. The need— chosen by many people— to be loved.

A need gone unrequited into the nights when television's troubled bars now and when in humbler homes Count John McCormack sounded in a programme of old music on a ricocheted radio.

2

May was always a strange month; one that either happened or didn't happen. This year it didn't happen, weather-wise, at the beginning.

It rained.

She looked through blurred windows.

She worked.

A Protestant minister's wife came to have a pink dress made for her daughter's wedding. Susan made it delightfully.

With floral embroidery. And afterwards the whole Protestant population of East Galway came to have their dresses made.

Dresses for weddings; summer frocks.

For the weather had lifted and now in the gardens of parsonages ministers' wives were young girls again among the apple-blossom.

Diarmaid— though he had not written— was far from her mind. It was as though she associated the events surrounding his home-coming and his not having written with bombs in England during the war. Something finally to be ignored.

As sunshine flowed she walked a lot alone and in the evenings— the martinets glowing— she did something she used never do before.

Watch television in the pub. Drink Guinness and listen to the troubled stories of passers-by.

But that wasn't all. She talked a lot to customers.

'Hello Mrs O'Hallrahan.'

The parson called one day looking for a dress for his daughter.

She was attending a garden-party in the Archbishop of Dublin's house.

'I'll bring her tomorrow so you can take measurements.'

'Grand.'

'How's your son?'

'He's in England.'

'Ah.' The man was kind. He questioned no further.

'You're looking lovely this weather, Mrs O'Hallrahan.'

'Ah. It's the sun.'

But she was. Darkened, softened by sun and bog breeze, her hair blown and darkened.

Smiling she returned the compliment.

'You're looking well yourself.'

Nimble as wish-bones he accepted the compliment.

'I wish you wouldn't make me feel too good.'

The man left.

She went on with her sewing.

In the afternoon she visited her mother, having bought blackened bananas for her.

2

Mrs Conlon bought a car and together they toured the countryside.

It was quite crazy. She could go anywhere now, Mrs Conlon could, and she did.

One day she travelled to Galway. Together they walked the pier at Salthill. It was a lovely, dazed blue sort of day.

And there was no-one about.

'It's lovely having a car,' Mrs Conlon said.

Susan agreed. 'It's good.' And she thought it particularly good that Mrs Conlon should invite her about so much.

Afterwards they had herring.

Travel is good for you, Mrs O'Hallrahan thought. Even if it's only to Galway.

Another day they visited Thoor Ballylea where the Irish poet, Yeats, lived.

It was a clear day and tinkers passed.

Red-haired tinkers.

They walked about.

Finding a swallow's nest in the ramparts.

Neither knew much about Yeats, but in this place Susan thought of her son. God bless him wherever he is, she thought.

Whatever he's doing.

3

She began having a little affair with the milkman.

She went out at night with him.

He drove her to Athlone.

There they saw 'Ryan's Daughter.'

The milkman— Mr Carey— wept at the end of it and to soothe him they entered a cafe.

The Genoa cafe.

There they had coffee and chips while the juke-box played moody young singers.

Around them Susan felt the eyes of young people. How funny they must seem to the young, Susan thought. Her dress was check. Blue and white.

A row commenced at another table. A girl hit a boy.

Tomato ketchup spilt.

It was like murder.

The girl walked off.

And she wondered, Susan did, what she was doing here with the milkman.

The voice on the juke-box sang, 'Bye, bye, Miss American Pie.'

She found the voice sweet and listened.

Singing 'This will be the day that I die' the voice ended.

Afterwards by the Shannon she walked with Matt Carey and felt deeply uncomfortable. She was a person, private.

She couldn't be going on dates with milkmen.

Before leaving her that night he asked for a further opportunity to see her.

'I'm not up to it,' she said. 'I'm not up to it.'

He sent a postcard.

The Tower of London on it.

It said 'Hi. I'm fine. How are you?   Got a job. Gave it up.
Auditioned for a part in a film. Didn't get it.

Goodbye. Diarmaid.'

He's mad, she thought. No address on it.

Where was he staying? What was he doing? Her mind
racked for an answer.

Didn't find it.

She was worried.

In a red check shirt she went to Mass the following Sunday.

A Mrs Hanratty approached her.

'We're forming a local women's organization. Would you
like to join?'

At first, startled, Susan asked,

'What kind of organization?'

'We'll grow flowers. Show old films. You know, the ones
you don't see now with Jeanette McDonald.

And go on hikes.'

It seemed improbable.

But she went to the first meeting. There an old lady spoke
about venial sin.

'It's all venial sin today. No mortal sin left. Life is gone
crazy; it's not lived any more. Let's be decisive. Let's be
mortal. Up with the women of the parish. Down with men.
We'll safeguard our own destiny. We'll lead on.'

She wanted to cry, Susan did. With laughter. It was so
funny. The lady— in black stockings— sounded as though
she'd never seen a man.

But all the same she went on one of the excursions, Mrs
O'Hallrahan did. To Limerick.

They visited the Treaty Stone, St John's Castle, had lemon
cake at the local ICA headquarters— demesne of a national
women's organization— and then left.

Up by Clare individual members of the party sang songs.
Numbers, rather crazy numbers. Like 'There's no business
like show business.'

When it came to Mrs O'Hallrahan's turn she sang 'Danny Boy.'

Light was leaving the sky. Castles stood out, Norman castles against the sea.

Stone walls collapsed, broken patterns. Some were bleached white. And here and there horses fused with the sunset, white tails.

And as she sang 'O Danny Boy, the pipes, the pipes are calling', a Spanish castle, perfect, spun by; a Spanish town, water bearing up ducks, swans, and a few boats.

As she finished she realized she'd made a big mistake. There was a huge silence in the bus.

Everybody, just about everybody, knew she was unknowingly singing about her son.

It was a song that pleased them, that pleased sentimental people.

It was a song which Susan had always considered perfect; a song of loveliness, of loss.

One she'd always associate with her husband and his singing of it in a ramshackle pub in Camden Town before he left for the war.

Now its truth horrified the occupants of the bus.

The love-song of a mother for her child.

Silence enveloped one Mrs Kileeney's blue hair. Across the hills of South Galway now a red sun shot through,a huge broken fire.

5

June was a lovely month. Early in the month the sun shone a lot; images froze.

Tinkers going by, the children's golden hair.

And one day with Mrs Conlon she went to Galway.

The sea was lovely. Both swam. Mrs Conlon looked like a turkey. Her backside was protruding, her legs a mesh of purple and blue.

Mrs O'Hallrahan looked almost elegant beside her.

Together they walked to the sea. Mrs O'Hallrahan felt the blue engulf her.

Come over her. Such blue it was. Blue over blue. She submerged herself; her body aimed against the waves.

And dipping her head she felt Diarmaid. Felt his presence today on this day that signified summer.

Her boy; a dream-boy. Like someone gone to war.

The June day was full of him. As she dried herself a blond boy ran past the sun.

Golden water-drops seeming to run off him.

As she gazed she was reminded of corn.

But then again it wasn't time for corn yet.

Later it would bleach the fields.

She walked away, towel in hand.

Life was so funny.

It was as though he were aching and nagging her.

Diarmaid.

She felt like a woman in love.

But more. Someone tempted by the world.

She looked around. It was so beautiful. Near to Galway was a light-house.

There she'd been first courted, Galway City before the war.

There her life had happened.

George, her husband, had brought her down alleys to meet shadows of Spanish lattices. Now it was happening again.

Her urge for living had returned.

She wanted to be near Diarmaid so much but felt his distance and the hours by train.

Should she go and see him? She played with the idea.

Visiting him now that it was summer.

But she let it go. Mrs Conlon was calling.

'Susie, I sprained my toe.'

6

Young hitch-hikers passed; the coming of summer at hand for them.

All shapes of rucksacks. Green. Orange. All shapes of faces and all colours of eyes.

Susan brooded on them. They all seemed so free, so fresh. So glad to be alive and on the road.

Some were obviously American; some French, others German. All trekking towards the beaches of Connemara of Clare.

All privileged. Yet something in her rejected their voyages. All were going the one path. Carelessly. Would they spend the rest of their lives travelling? Would the spirit of participation and conquest always be present in them? Or would they just give up?

George, her husband, never gave up. In a way she hadn't either. But this generation treked on with a lot of money to a destination they weren't sure of. Then she thought of Diarmaid and tenderness filled her.

They were in need of a goal.

She placed plates on the table for a solitary lunch. Bread and butter. She was alone. Still a girl in a sense. Always watching out and eager.

Still hopeful.

Beside the school, hidden under glass, was a statue of the Blessed Virgin. White and blue. She looked out at it. Young people passed it, anoraks.

A very beautiful blond boy went by. His hair was long.

He walked with grace; his jeans were the colour of ink when faded on blotting paper in the school she once went to. His face was shaped almost like a ewe's.

Pale, too, like a ewe's. And his eyes were keen and blue. Markedly blue.

To the point of mad and unnecessary beauty.

She wished him well on his journey. Quietly her mouth paused on the tea.

And her thoughts travelled past images of flying German bombers to an image of she and her husband before the war, sitting on steps leading down to the Claddagh in Galway, feet dipping in water. Her dress had been pink. Her feet pale.

He'd looked sideways at her, George had.

Took her foot, kissed it, his hair blond.

'You've lovely feet,' he told her.

And she realized, even at her desperately young age, how few people in Ireland would ever have said something like that.

They'd been convicted by history, neutralized by the church.

Watching a blond Swedish boy now— her mind told her he was Swedish— she thought of this moment.

Because— because— within a flash inside her— she felt desire. She rose, stroked her hair.

A phrase of Diarmaid's returned. 'Too much.'

Yes it was all too much. She could hear again the music of crossroad balls, when she was young.

Feel the shadows on the roadway.

Dresses funnily twirling and lights shining like a gospel of madness in this generally unlively Irish environment.

In the afternoon she cycled to deliver a dress.

People passed, said hello. She gazed at a cloud.

And her legs freshened towards an old damnation hymn. She was young, fresh, in need of love.

Hope, companionship.

7

John stayed one night only. He was Canadian; from Montreal. It had been raining; she'd taken him in.

Over Weetabix he'd spoken of French Canada, comparing it to Ireland. He spoke of a Jewish confectioner who'd run off with his mother.

She fried sausages, ham, cooked chicken. He ate. She

watched, mad with caution. Going to bed that night she glimpsed his nakedness through an open door and went to sleep with that image.

8

'Diarmaid, why don't you write?' she wrote, care of his aunt. No reply. She wrote to his aunt. Yes, he'd collected the letter. He was living with hippies the aunt declared. He must be rescued.

But she was making a garment for a French lady who'd come to live in Ballinasloe. She couldn't for the moment care less.

Delicately she threaded it together. Then one night— it was Midsummer— she realized how she missed Diarmaid.

Entering his room she found an ikon of a boy, his mouth spilling blood. She'd never noticed it with such intensity before. 'Diarmaid.' It was as though she were appealing to a ghost.

'Diarmaid.' A shadow crossed the room.

And at the same time a shadow crossed her mind. She wanted to see her son.

1

She crossed in the ship 'Hibernia. Her dress had pink patterns. She sat, arms folded, grimly listening to pop-music until a man shook her arm and said 'Mam, don't look so gloomy.'

Apparently he was doing it to many women because already he seemed to have done it to an old lady, sitting up smiling, awaiting his attentions.

'Come and join us.' She did. He took out a fiddle and began playing. A lady and gentleman got up and danced. A reel. Over the ship's cafeteria. And the man shouted with glee.

Then another man joined him. 'How are you, Pat?' he greeted the man.

'Fine.'

'Give us an old song.' The ship quietened. A woman who looked as though she'd been vomiting became quite silent. A bruised damaged look about her eyes. She listened, even as the waves seemed to have to.

The man sang 'She is far from the land.'

A song every Irishman knew was about Robert Emmet's love, Sarah Curran. The story of her life after his death. 'She is far from the land where her young here sleeps.'

Quietly a man puffed a cigar.

Softly a lady's face lighted up.

The man continued:-

'He had lived for his love, for his country he died.

They were all that to life had entwined him.

Nor soon shall the tears of his country be dried,

Nor long will his love stay behind him.'

They could almost hear the left-over, disgorged sounds of Ireland.

A curlew's cry; a train's bleat. The flashing of Guinness across a crowded pub— these the sights— a wet rainy tricolour flapping in the wind. They could feel these things, hear them, see them.

The boat was slightly out-of-date. It was 1972.

Time had passed the island by but still somewhere the voice of these things landed on a pavement in Camden Town.

Ireland was still unfree, still unwound.

Still hopelessly, narcissistically in love with itself, like a virgin who'd never let up and knew now her last lover, her last chance of a lover, had just cycled up the laneway. The voice over, the song quelled, someone was ignorant enough to put on a Stevie Wonder on the juke-box, and the pop-singer's voice became the voice of ignorance, of farawayness, of young men in Belfast shooting the faces of old men and young men for the cause of match-sticks. For the cause of what was in effect almost nothing any more.

They spoke, the Irish contingent.

Two women, one Mrs O'Hallrahan. Two men. One who'd played the fiddle, the other who'd sung. They spoke.

Voices roaring about them, waves turning.

The other lady began.

Her nose had the intense look of a hen; crooked glasses on it. Her dress was flavoured with a sort of very dark colour.

'My son was eighteen when he left home. He was a dark-haired country lad.

My only son, His father hoped he'd take over the farm. He didn't want to. He went to London and became a bus-conductor. Then he got tired of that; joined the Navy. Went to foreign parts. Sometimes we'd hear from him. Sometimes months would go by without word.

And all the time I'd pray.

Then eventually he got fed up of that, too; bought a business in London, settled down. He married a West Indian girl. She left him after a month. This we found out. Strangely enough on a visit to the North of England our only son killed himself from the top of a gas-works. From a railing or something.'

It was a strange story. One which made little sense to Susan.

They all began to talk about death then; about brothers and sisters and uncles who'd committed suicide.

The woman apparently was going to settle up some business of her late son's. A sad task.

One of the men was going to retrieve a daughter who'd run away from home. The other was quietly seeking a wife who'd left him. All the same story. Closely bound up.

They seemed drawn together by a mandate.

All seemed to be looking at Susan to know why she was going to England.

She said nothing at first.

She looked from one to the other and said simply, 'My son is lost to me, too. Just eighteen. He's over in England, too. He won't write to me.

But I'm worried.

Sometimes I'm afraid lest something will happen to him. It's funny. I know you shouldn't think like that but I can't help it. I need to find him soon before it's too late.'

'Too late?' the woman questioned her.

'Too late. Yes. Before he's gone from me forever.' That said, Susan relexed. She'd spoken more forthrightly than ever she'd spoken before.

Like a balloon burst at a maidenly party long ago. There was nothing else to be said.

2

Her company was strange.

This she realized.

Formal— like a sacrament— the people sat around. The men played cards. A flower on the other woman's hat drooped. Like an angel in retirement.

All was not lost, Susan told herself. Yet as dawn blurred she experienced strangeness beyond belief.

As though this was not happening now. As though it had happened long ago. There was something graceful, yet something sinister about it.

It was like a dance of death.

Afterwards she had no idea how she got into those people's company, but as she walked out of Euston Station she remembered how the man with the fiddle had played a reel towards seven o' clock in the morning and shouted:-

'Never let it get you down, Ma'am.' Slapping Susan's knee. 'This is a world built of sorrow, but there's no need to give in to sorrow.

What's here today is gone tomorrow.

So forget about it all.'

And when people were drifting off the boat he was still eulogizing his native Clare and the gulls over a castle built by the Spaniards and destroyed —with the burning of a few bishops— by Cromwell's men.

That morning London was cold. It rained. Sombrely.

Susan had no wish to think.

She got a taxi to her sister in Ladbroke Grove.

3

She had to press a bell. Her sister— or rather her sister-in-law (sister was a more desirable term)— Bridget, answered.

'Darling.' She had big lips. Like an umbrella. Red.

A cigarette hung from her fingers. 'Sweet-heart.'

They kissed.

Embraced.

Like two prostitutes.

'Well you're looking great, Bridget.'

'You're lovely yourself, Susan.'

Bridget picked up Susan's hair.

'I remember George once saying you had hair like blackberries.

Well you still have. And sure you've a face like a star.

What have you been doing?' Bridget touched Susan; her finger probed Susan's left breast like a magic wand. Her voice rang with devilment, as they would say at home.

'Have you been having an affair?'

Susan was seated on a red chair under a picture of a Geisha girl.

Sherry was produced. It flavoured the room.

'You're so worried about Diarmaid, aren't you. He sometimes comes here-- looking like God only knows what.

I haven't seen him for a while, but I know his address because he was expecting a letter here from some friend in the North.'

Susan's lips opened. She was only delighted as she would have said herself. Thrilled to know that she would soon see her son.

Bridget prepared lunch. She worked as a char-lady-- part-time. She wasn't working today and she prepared a meal. Roast potatoes floated before Susan, pork chops. A little canister of apple-sauce. It was such a good meal that Susan forgot about time and soon it was evening.

Too late to look for Diarmaid, Susan realized. So half-gladly Susan drifted into conversation. Over sherry. The sherry had a twilit, faraway look in it. Faintly it glowed. She talked about Diarmaid, Susan did. How she loved him and worried about him. What was he doing? What was he up to? And she voiced the fear that he might be on drugs. Bridget listened intently.

'Yes. He has that look,' Bridget said. As though trying to arouse more fear. Though basically Susan couldn't have cared less. She wasn't worried about drugs. It was more a worry that Diarmaid had gone from her for ever. Drifted off as sheep did in Spring from the hills in East Galway. Going before nightfall to some untold destination. And as the image of sheep filled her mind so also the often maimed sheep-like expression of Diarmaid, pale, fleshless, wounded.

The look on his face weeks after Derek O'Mahony had killed himself. The look of hurt. Of dismay. Sometimes almost even of revenge. His eyes narrowing to the memory of Derek O'Mahony. Like burnt-out buildings. Some day she often felt then he was going to do something terrible, though what terrible thing he could do she didn't know.

Bridget persisted in talking. Talking on and on. The sleeve of her dress drooped a little.

She was a lonely woman. Never married. Living life in the parlours of rich Londoners, paid to mind children, to peel tomatoes. Once a child she was very attached to was burned in a hotel fire in Portugal, and in a way she never recovered from that. She continued, bore up, a sort of postscript in her family.

George, she spoke of him, now forgetting how long dead he was.

Her words flowed. Quickly.

She spoke of growing up with him, the toys her father would bring home from a fair in Mullingar.

And it occurred to Susan how passionately sad a person George had been, fleeing from place to place, landing himself in a war, eventually landing himself in an elevator in Chicago.

The misfortunes of war had had little effect on him; he was fearless she often thought, guarded totally against the world, its way, heading along to an inevitable death. And she felt sometimes— now even— that he was a stranger to her, lost in the web of her solitude, brusquely forgotten.

Diarmaid was much nearer, like the cracked bit in a mirror. One's own reflection, a broken commodity, something that reflected her, her images, world, dreams, much closer than a far-forgotten death approximate to a Saint Patrick's Day in 1954 when girls marched in the rain, shamrocks swollen like hankies about their breasts.

'George.' She tried to sum up his name that night. His sister bore some resemblance to him. The long face, cordial expression, chin that stuck out. As though pinching something.

Her lipstick faded now, Bridget talked on.

Her knowledge of Diarmaid was obviously slight. She pretended distress but obviously there was little she could identify with in a boy who sometimes came, went, disappeared probably without a word of thanks for lunch.

Curtains were pulled; London shut out.

Bit by bit the conversation petered out.

Perhaps because Susan was contemplating the face that Bridget understood so little.

In fact she, Bridget, probably expected that Susan was only here on a weird, fifty-year-old— womanish holiday.

That wasn't the truth. No-one knew the truth as much as she when she confronted the mirror that night. Light cracked through. Hoarsely.

In the mirror she saw herself. Her face old, forehead pale with light but still there the freshness George had loved her for. She stood— like something she'd just conjured herself— the light still off.

Then offsetting romanticism and the last few moments with Bridget she put on the light but the effect was even more tender. Rouge the lamp lit.

She was seized, almost infuriated by the glow. She was alive, well, on the eve of what, a visit to her son.

She was going to seek him out. 'He's in very strange company,' Bridget had said at one stage. 'He arrived here one day with a strange-looking lady. A girl with red lipstick and eyes that were painted all colours.' Susan hadn't thought about it. Now she did.

Was Diarmaid in love again? Was he thinking of her, Susan, or engaging in some adolescent love-affair? The more she thought of it the more she wanted to cry.

Diarmaid, her son, was living apart from her. Away. She pronounced the word. Mentally.

What had happened? Why was she here? What was she pursuing?

Nothing.

Blankly she looked towards the London street. Outside figures trouped; no end to loneliness.

George. Like a mask she accepted the memory of his face, George, her young man of the late thirties. And yet what was real about their relationship but a nostalgic moment? And the disturbed tragic happening on his face in the fifties when he knew it was over, pursuit.

In a way Diarmaid revived reality in a more forceful way in her; he was of the grim earth.

She knew this. From his ikons she knew his compassion and his need to construct. Away somewhere in a County Galway night he'd been struck with wonder. Held on to that amazement.

Life indeed for him was amazing. Even if Bridget didn't understand it; didn't understand the love-affair of a young boy with himself.

4

That night she didn't sleep very well. In fact she slept rather badly and it occurred to her that Bridget was continually going to the toilet, her ghost trailing out.

Usually a friend slept in the room Susan was sleeping in. That other lady, ex-Irish too, was now on a holiday in Cornwall, St Ives.

A postcard hung over the Sacred Heart in the kitchen, a view of churches sweeping down to the sea.

Sometimes, too, Diarmaid had slept in this bed, the lady away with friends in the country.

Susan imagined him arriving at the door; hair washed over his forehead, telling her he saw a boy die from heroin, and she wondering simply. Tonight she was glad of Bridget's company, but nothing was understood of broken statues of the Blessed Virgin in East Galway and the need for a son.

She obviously had a sick stomach, Bridget had. Continually the toilet flushed and in the small hours, hauntingly Susan glimpsed Diarmaid walking past a chip shop, and in her mind his image was confused with her young friend of the late thirties, a grocer's assistant, the one who'd died in Durham, grounded there in the late forties, working as a gardener. Diarmaid had always reminded her of him, this white-headed boy who'd fleeted in and out of her life and

84

whom she remembered, when small, completing transfers from half-penny lucky bags.

He'd lived near her, only going to Galway when he was seventeen. Cabbages, rainbows on cauliflowers; they returned from his grocery shop in Galway when she woke.

She thought of him; intensely, just a boy who was a friend in between the love-relationship with George.

She went to the window. An old lady passed. Trampishly hair sticking out. Blue. Even in the night light.

And she wondered what she was doing. Picking up bits and pieces of life, mending them— like wounded crows. George, this boy, David, in Galway in the late thirties, Diarmaid. Snatching some intensity from people's eyes; going about a life as aimless and as driftless as geese. What had happened to her? Where was the security and the peace of mind which once had been? Gone with Diarmaid's entry into the world; his whole questioning position had wrought havoc on her. She stood now like a stupid virgin on a dance-hall floor.

Nowhere really to go. Tomorrow— Friday in fact— she was going to raid Diarmaid's life. For what? Maybe— sincerely— just to know how he was.

5

Buses crept past; London's red buses. Bridget called her. 'Get up, love. I've your breakfast ready.'

It was a lovely breakfast; toast, marmalade, apple-jelly. There was a look of pain on Bridget's brow and it occurred to Susan that she genuinely suffered; somewhere in the night fear took her.

Fear of what, Susan didn't know. Over breakfast remarks continued from the previous night; Bridget discovered a bottle of wine, opened it. 'Wine for breakfast.' Her voice was shrill. Susan was aghast. Something was happening in Bridget's head. This Susan was sure of now.

They cleaned up things. Both were slightly drunk and

apparently none the worse for it.

The address Bridget had given Susan was Endsleigh Gardens. Bridget directed her as to how to get there. She took it, Susan did, in a sort of stupour, Bridget going to a late rendez-vous with some woman for whom she cleaned up.

A red bus took Susan to Euston Square. From there she walked to Endsleigh Gardens. The door was white. No-one was in. She knocked many times.

Last night's roses came back; some perched on a shining table in Bridget's sitting-room, a statue of the Blessed Virgin, a picture of Pope Pius the Tenth; saintly, haloed in gold. All these bits of Irishness, random bits of emigration, singular in Susan's mind now.

Bits of disillusion. She walked away.

But not before she concentrated on the image of a cat she once used maul as a child. She felt so empty, so lifeless, so much the prey of others.

For a moment it was as though there was nothing to the world, nothing to life; that one always had to become just another person.

A bag of disillusion, emptiness. So she wanted to concentrate desperately on some image of importance to her; so she thought of the cat, far back.

A cat. She held the whole world close to her in the image of that cat.

She wanted so much to love things. Yet here she was walking down a street called Fitzroy Street. Crying almost.

'Are you lonesome tonight? Do you miss me tonight?' Words from a jaded song returned; the remarks on radio at home. Nights when Galway welled about her and she felt like ascending, levitating, doing anything to get away, feel apart. She walked slowly.

As one walked at a funeral at home. God.

An old lady picked up a paper and read the headlines. Something about a bomb in Belfast.

That ended her day. She sat in a restaurant, drank coffee. Her eyes poured out, questioned the paradise of moments outside. Lovely people, stately legs, dream-blue jeans. Summer in progress, the light moments. And here was she, Susan O'Hallrahan, widow, deeply wanting in common-sense, sitting on board at a tragedy. For that's the way she felt it now. It was all tragic, dimensionless, drifting.

She had no home. No future. She was so alone, deserted, betrayed by death, by her son, even now by her ordinary day to day common-sense.

'Red pepper soup, a woman beside her ordered. Time to go. She rose and left— with such punch to make young men look at her. A picture-postcard of Mick Jagger swept by her — her son's hero, notable in a trance.

Home that evening Bridget was crying.

'I'm dead worried,' she said. 'I'm afraid sometimes I have cancer.'

'Cancer.' The word went back in Susan's mind. 'Where?' 'In my left breast.'

'What makes you think that?'

'Nights. Sleepless nights and a pain here that couldn't be anything else. It feels like cancer. Even if I don't know what cancer is.'

Susan took her hand.

'Bridget, love, don't worry. We'll go to a doctor tomorrow to dispel your fears.'

They did. But the doctor wasn't hopeful. Within a few days it was confirmed. She had all the marks of cancer. They did many things together, went to the ballet. June, July merged; summer was a feeling that travelled quickly and remotely through London thoroughfares.

At the end of these days though Susan trudged again to Euston Square and Endsleigh Gardens.

This time music moved inside; loud sounds; a girl opened the door. Liquid hair dangled, tenuous golds and brown. She admitted Susan.

'I'm Diarmaid O'Hallrahan's mother', she said. 'Is he here?'

Over the fireplace a young boy fondled a kitten. Susan recognised Christ dangling. But the picture was remote; Susan recognised it as a mockery of the event, felt obliged to feel some sort of distaste. But it was short-lived.

Here was a sitting Buddah.

There was a picture of an Indian temple. And a girl-singer's photograph hung over the mantlepiece, small.

'He's not here. He went North yesterday. Take a seat.'

These are the voices she heard. She took no notice of them. She felt her heart throbbing. This was unreal to her; these were the young people who traipsed past her window, in blue jeans, to destinations in Connemara. 'God.' She sat down. After a minute she recovered voice.

'Could you turn down the music, please?'

Promptly they obeyed. She sounded tougher than ever she had before. She felt like addressing them as brats.

Then she wanted more information.

'Gone North with who?'

'A guy,' the girl said.

Susan peered. Yes, this girl had been Diarmaid's lover.

She knew it from the shape of her eyes, her complexion; everything had a bit of Diarmaid.

'Will you have coffee?'

A boy with hair like a polar bear's asked.

She looked at him with surprise.

'O.K.'

They made her a mug of coffee and offered her a bun.

One with a cherry on it. The girl said she'd made them.

Her name was Alice.

Gradually the others introduced themselves. This was a kind of commune. The first Susan had come upon. She looked about in disbelief. So these were the sort of people Diarmaid was mixing with.

This was his world.

And after a minute or two the strangeness wore off and the events of the past few days seemed to implant a new honesty in Susan, Bridget and all that. She could only see these people remotely— maybe as they were— disconnected from reality.

Reality was life's pounding wounds. Like Bridget's face on previous nights. Waiting death like a swan on Irish waters — one of those ancient holy creatures of Ireland who inhabited its lake towards evening.

Anyway the music which had invaded Susan's ears as she thought of swans and Bridget had been the music of 'Swan Lake' at the ballet the other night.

There were no real coincidences. Everything was bound up.

Everything.

She saw a picture of Mick Jagger on a magazine cover, her son's elusive hero whose name she sometimes remembered and sometimes forgot. But there he was again. She felt like chastising him.

'And who are ye? Diarmaid's friends.'

She'd never sounded so raucously Irish.

'Yes.'

They were meek in their replies.

'How long did Diarmaid live here?'

'Oh on and off.'

'And where's this friend of his and himself gone?'

'To York,' came the quick reply.

'York, God save us.'

'His friend lectures there.'

'Lectures?'

'Yes, he's an economics lecturer.'

That was new. That was sudden.

The boy in a green shirt told her. His nose had a tremendous resemblance to Pope Paul's.

Alice, the girl, stirred.

'Are you hungry?'

'No, no love.'

And she recognised the look on the face, a look like Diarmaid's, as familiar as the portion of stained glass in the church at home. She felt almost — yes, the word was compassion. She felt strongly for the child. Her son, her daughter.

She recognised that moment— strangely— that this girl

must have been a lover of Diarmaid.

'O Sacred Heart of Jesus I place all my trust in Thee.' Words from a chapel at home.

They returned. Her vision was complete. Here Diarmaid used sleep with this girl.

She had more coffee. 'Two, please.' She asked for sugar. She was becoming more interested. The 'Peace News' lay beside here. Above her a poster of an atom bomb exploding, a mushroom of smoke with a child emerging from it.

Strange. And she wondered what someone like Mrs Conlon would think of all this.

They talked, dribs and drabs of conversation, as Susan would say herself.

Bits of nothing passed between them.

Cherries were produced; they delicately picked them from a mauve bowl. And all the time Susan was noticing Alice, the namesake of her niece, sitting beside the Buddah. An expression half of curiosity, half of faith in her eyes. She wanted to know more. So did Susan.

She held on, Susan did. One boy was going out to buy cabbage. Another was off to see an old house he and friends of his were thinking of occupying. Altogether Susan was alone now with Alice, apart from a cat and a youth who painted in another room.

'Where did you get your shoes?' the girl asked.

'Why, in Galway.'

'They're lovely.'

Big and boorish, Susan thought.

Black. She found herself gazing down.

And between them the shoes stood, a barrier.

'Did you know Diarmaid well?'

'O.K. Well enough.'

'What sort of form is he in?'

'Well as can be expected.'

The girl sounded bitter underneath, betrayed. She had on a red check shirt.

It flowed about her hips which were neat and tapering.

90

Bluntly her knees knocked together.

'I haven't seen him for a few days. I left this place before he left. When I came back he was gone.'

'Where to? Oh yes. The North.

Good God. What brought him there?'

'His friend. Michael.'

Susan was perplexed. Who was this man? What was he doing in Diarmaid's life. From the way Alice spoke of him she gauged that he was young. Or somehow intense enough to be taken for young.

She wondered about him. Alice kept talking.

'Diarmaid's been behaving very strangely recently.'

'How strangely?'

Susan wanted to question quickly, immediately. Now it was coming back.

The emptiness of the last days was going for an acute, almost apostolic awareness of Diarmaid; he was a case-history, Diarmaid was. Case of what? Of strange and unwanted feelings. They were her feelings, too; her strength.

Something she'd never suffered for as much as he, but something of which she was totally aware.

The nerve-system of a country. Here she had it in the palm of her hand, Diarmaid's relationship with Derek O'Mahony. Alice was another Derek O'Mahony. She wanted to ask Alice many questions, but couldn't. The girl looked strained.

'In other words,' she said after a few minutes, 'I was in love with Diarmaid and he left me.'

She was beginning to cry but something— perhaps recognising the fellowship of Susan— stopped her. She took in Diarmaid's mother.

'You must think I'm awful saying this, but I really loved Diarmaid.

But he's so messed up.

There was nothing I could do. He wanted me so much. Then suddenly he left me. He must have changed his mind and I-- like a fool— realized I cared more for him than for anybody before. He was like a God to me. He was the nicest guy I've met. Tender. That's it. But his tenderness didn't seem to stretch when I needed it.'

All was a bit confusing but it was all there, the long ago at school, Derek O'Mahony wanting Diarmaid, but Diarmaid— finally— being unable to give himself. Tied up in the back of his mind with rabbits— these he would play with as a child— and yes, her, Susan.

Their relationship exact, living; their daily choice when he had knots of livid hair.

The girl spoke on. 'I hope you don't consider me foolish.'

'Anyway, getting back to the point,' Susan said, 'what about this man Diarmaid's gone away with?'

'Michael. He's crazy. He'll drive Diarmaid into a mental asylum yet.'

'What do you mean?'

But before she could answer a boy came in. He looked at Susan, then looked at Alice, began playing a piano in another room. Shortly after that more batches of people arrived and all— apparently taken by Susan's brogue— began treating her as though she were a rare and welcome visitor. A girl with dyed hair wailed with laughter at a joke Susan made about the frost.

'Yes it's cold in winter where I live and frost covers the road at night. You'd swear every donkey passing was Jack the Ripper.'

She couldn't believe her own words. She was going crazy. She wanted to leave.

'Listen,' Alice said. 'Here's Diarmaid's address in York.'

Alice handed it to Susan though Susan wasn't sure what she was supposed to do about it.

'Goodbye, love.'

'Goodbye.'

She was glad to be on the street again and away from people she didn't quite understand.

6

Bridget sat up in bed that night. 'If I were you I'd take a decent holiday. Get away from the city. It's no good. I've spent half my life here. Now it's dead for me and I'm dying.

And I won't go home either before I die. I've given my life to this place and here I'll stay.'

'But I live in the country,' Susan said.

'You've never seen England though, have you?'

'Yes, I've been around.'

Yet the idea struck her.

Maybe she should visit a country place in Britain.

'Will you come?' she asked Bridget in the morning.

The refusal was solid.

Where would she go?

Suggestions escaped her.

Maybe, maybe she thought she should go to York to see Diarmaid.

But of that she was afraid.

Who was this man he was living with?

On a Tuesday she met Alice outside a shop.

'I had a postcard from Diarmaid. He's happy.'

One that bewildered Susan altogether. Diarmaid happy. Yes, she'd go to investigate.

7

She'd never really been to many places but this could have been Venice, Florence to her. Boys in white trousers, their hair very blond and glowing, walked by.

She felt an immediate intimacy, an immediate glow inside herself even.

The Cathedral opened, a huge structure. It seemed to fold the streets in; take them into itself. The town indeed was a wonder.

She didn't move. Just sat on a bench by the river as evening came. Young men canoed; colours drifted. All was complete.

If she had a thousand sons she didn't feel like seeing them now. Let them go about their lives. She was herself now. She didn't need sons.

But she headed to Diarmaid's address.

Drawn there out of no particular compulsion.

It all seemed so mindless now. The detective politics of looking for Diarmaid were over.

Let him go his life, she felt. She had no wish to interfere. When she arrived the door was red; the house part of riverside mews.

Inside light was on, curtains drawn, shielding the windows.

A young man answered.

About twenty-four. He looked as though he could have been older.

His face lean, taut, eyes shooting out like little fires.

His hand lay on the door-knob. He looked— quite honestly Susan thought later— like a frightened child.

'I'm Diarmaid's mother. I'm staying in a hotel nearby. I just popped around to see him.' It was a crazy lie. She had nowhere to stay. Her bags were at the station. She felt like a hippie.

'He's not here. He went yesterday.'

Again now she realized how much she wanted to see him. It had never occurred to her, the importance of her venture.

She felt cold, betrayed. She'd wanted to see Diarmaid. Even if it was as if she couldn't care earlier.

But caring was with her all the time. She'd tried to pretend cynicism. She wanted just to be herself, a woman, but now she realized she wanted and needed Diarmaid so much. She was utterly fed up of pretending.

'Can I come in? I'm tired.'

She stepped in. The house was covered with pictures. Mainly reproductions of little boys painted by apparently famous painters.

'Sorry. I should have invited you earlier. I hope I didn't appear rude.'

'No.'

94

Susan sat down. She wanted to sleep on something. She couldn't care what this strange man thought.

'I feel so tired.'

'Do you wish to sleep?'

Alarmed at his generosity she looked at him.

'Yes please.' Her head was swooming. Something which held her together was gone. All the ropes, and in her mind she could see the trapeze artist she'd viewed with Diarmaid, a symbol, and also now the train journeys of her life, those over the bridge in Ballinasloe, one to Dublin to meet George's remains.

She felt like crying. Rolling up like a teething child.

This was it; her moment. She'd never go back now.

She cared passionately for Diarmaid.

She'd wanted to show him that by coming to the green parts of England to meet him.

The young man, Michael, showed her to her room. There she curled up. Inside her there was fear. Bloated. It must have been like a miscarriage.

In the night she woke up. Instead of blood there were tears on the pillow.

She'd been crying. Though in a way there was little to cry at in her life. She'd wept at George's departure; in Dublin she'd stood motionless as George's body was produced from an aeroplane.

Then wailed like women used when she was a child and met coffins on country roads and keened them.

The tears on her pillow now were an aftermath of the last years; Diarmaid's subjectivity, his experiences at school, the lonesomeness of school-days.

It was also her lonesomeness.

This she realized. Outside was a new moon. A singular loveliness about the night.

'Your troubles are my troubles'. In her head she was calling Diarmaid. Am I going mad? The thought occurred to her. Would they lock her up and put her in an asylum? Maybe. A mad lady she was now, going to ballets in London, traipzing about like a harlot, talking to herself.

But all this was beside the point.

A cat sneaked by.

Her breath softened the window-pane. Blurred.

In the glamour it was Galway again.

She and George, making amends for their sadness, their individual solitude, making love in a barn. All these years she'd forgotten, she'd forgotten because she hadn't cared. George and she had made love before they married. A terrible sin in Irish consciousness; in fact there'd been pilgrimages to Lourdes against it, prayers at Fatima, and in Ireland's own shrine, Knock, they'd invoked Mary Magdalene and John the Baptist against sex. But she and George had done it. They hadn't cared. They hadn't confessed it. They'd married. Now all the young people in Ireland were making love.

But it came to her as an outstanding revelation that she and George had openly defied all codes; there in a barn outside Galway, tide swollen in the nearby sea, she'd kissed his lips and bent to his organ, as innocent and lifeless at first as that of a stone cupid. She'd woken him.

Much shame should have poured on her. It didn't. After they'd married— years after the war— they'd gone to the October Fair in Ballinasloe. Lights lovely, colourful, and there as Betty Grable sang a raucous song over the loud-speaker she saw a girl call out her lover's name. That had been the last time she'd remembered her first act of sex with George. Now recalling it beauty filled the night— York Minster stood out.

'Diarmaid.' His plight had begun that night in Galway. That night— though he didn't come for many years later— his existence was devoted to truth.

8

Over the next few days they became like a couple setting up house together, Susan and Michael. It was strange,

96

possibly the strangest point of her life. They knew one another quickly; they grabbed easily. Walking around York he bought her a cerise blouse— Michael had been Diarmaid's friend. This she gathered bit by bit.

Over porridge, wheat-germ on the porridge, he told her about Diarmaid's coming here. They'd met in London.

In the flat at Endsleigh Gardens. Michael had been there with his wife-to-be, Eleanor. Both friends of one of the occupants. But they hadn't been getting on too well.

The night there they'd finally broken up. Eleanor had gone into the street, Michael following her.

It was over; she wept. Upper-English, used to gardens, she hadn't really accepted Michael though they'd been away together. Spent a summer North of Venice. He was Yorkshire, pained-looking; she'd been used to parsonages, couldn't accept something in him.

Maybe bluntness, blue jeans.

She'd listened whimsically to all this, Susan had.

What was the world coming to? Young people everywhere fighting.

Though she knew their fighting was special, was part of their attachment.

In her mind Susan envisaged a girl in a pale frock; it was like listening to an old film retold, listening to Michael. He set a scene, almost described clothes exactly.

'We'd seemed so much in love. But no, it was over. We just couldn't get on any more.'

'And where does Diarmaid fit into the picture?'

'That morning Eleanor got a cab, saying she was going to her brother in Cyprus. She claimed it was definitely over because I hit her. I did. When she was screaming at me about my appearance. Aspects of it didn't appeal to her.

She sat down— sobbing. "I can't have this. I can't have this," she screamed. But basically she was saying we were no longer in love. Or worse, never had been. Were relying on one another.

I walked home.

Diarmaid was standing at the door. His fists were knotted together.

He looked like a Greek god or something.

Something cut out of stone; always there. Yet somewhat tender-looking.

I was crying. I must have looked like a red-looking rhinoceros. I was weeping loudly.

Diarmaid just came up to me— Michael was hesitant— put his arm about me and said quietly 'You'll be O.K.'

That afternoon we went to the Victoria and Albert Museum together.

It was something I won't forget.'

His arms were brown.

She was sitting on a cushion, feeling very comfortable, but most ungraceful.

Yet she was happy, strangely happy. Like a young girl.

Someone who'd recovered youth, beauty, and didn't know what to do with it.

Eleanor seemed to have been just a slot in Michael's life; this Susan gauged. Like white roses over a garden wall she'd passed by, a delicacy, nothing more. Here now, Michael was alive, disgruntled, young, afraid.

She felt like saying something like 'sow' to him, but that would have been disastrous, unhealthy; she felt like a mother to him. But also now acting adviser.

It was a strange mixture of bodies. The two on the floor, facing one another. Involved in what? – getting to know divisions.

'He came here to get away from London.

He was fed up of the girl he was living with, Alice. She was getting on his nerves.

To me she was a lovely girl, just out of school, knowing little or nothing about the world. But she was familiar with certain drugs. In convent school apparently she'd over-dosed herself with barbiturates, which event had immediate associations for Diarmaid, seeing I think that a friend of his died at school. They were both products of Catholic environments. They had nothing to lose and much to identify with in one another.

And when the crunch came they were lovers.

The flat they'd been staying in was vaguely run by pacifists. Another great cause to their very young and tender minds.

But finally it didn't work; the protest marches, the letters to embassies, the drugs— ', Michael hesitated on this word, 'it was all too ready-made. Their relationship disintegrated. Diarmaid left with me for York.'

Susan couldn't help feeling she was getting very matter-of-fact treatment; like a report on the Stock Exchange on television. But she listened. It was all new to her and she listened, picking out the bits of Diarmaid's life, unsurprised at Michael's frankness, but wondering. Wondering at where it was all leading to— this openness.

They walked about York. Susan saw an old lady with cherries in her bonnet; a yacht sail under a bridge. All calm it pushed forward. And she was totally overtaken by these things.

She was wearing white shoes now, big ones. Her dress blue, hair blown and her features were tanned. Altogether it was enough to make young men look at her.

She'd smile, passing them, Michael giving almost a jealous stare.

This was her moment— she recognised it— it had come.

Life could pass by now— calmly. Like the yacht. It was over. She'd reached something. At fifty-three she was lovely. Lovely enough to attract attention in a street in York, to invite the inquisitiveness of a young man like Michael.

What would Mrs Conlon think now? And all the Mrs Conlons?

She'd changed so much. This she thought on looking into a shop-window one day. It was an antique shop-window, old furniture inside. But maybe it was that she hadn't changed, but that she'd become herself again. And she thought of a night after the war when she visited the men's social club in

Ballinasloe with George. Inside were billiard tables; people playing, old photographs, brown almost. While her husband played snooker she watched the trees outside. They were so green.

She concentrated on them, images of war returning, and she felt renewal. The trees were leafy, full of green. Next week she'd heard they were going to be cut down.

She felt like going and stopping it, but there was nothing to be done.

They were cut down and as the fair came to Ballinasloe only old stumps were left.

Her bewilderment returned to her now as she stared at her image. More than bewilderment. Fright.

But she was calm now. She knew the years had peeled away like wall-paper, that here she was as a girl in Galway; totally responsive.

There wasn't a further path to travel. She remembered walking with Diarmaid in Spring and felt now the presence of Autumn, the year pivoting. She'd never been more herself than now. It was over, her truth.

She turned about and seemed to gaze into the eyes of a young girl, arms touched by freckles, in Galway, 1939.

9

Michael enjoyed her meals; rainbow trout, buttered potatoes. The trout came from Scotland.

'I imagine Ireland to be very like Scotland,' Michael said over the rainbow trout.

'I don't know. I'd say it's softer somehow.'

'My parents used go to Scotland all the time when I was young. To a cottage near a lake. There I'd read Charles Dickens —.' He searched Susan's face to know if she knew of Charles Dickens —.' It was very pleasant. Other times I'd go down to the lake and find the land covered with dead eels and I'd run back in terror. My father and mother were just

about to break up at the time and one day, naked, I saw my
father beat my mother. Later when I was twelve or fourteen
I had dreams of dead eels and my father beating my mother,
naked, and my whole head would reel with dead eels which
were somehow my father's private parts.

Susan had a fit of uncontrollable laughter. Then—
suddenly— she ceased, realizing it wasn't altogether funny.

'I think Diarmaid was a bit like that, too. He used have
awful nightmares once.'

'But the worst,' Michael said, 'is that school. He hated it.
I don't think he'll ever recover from it. The boy hanging
himself and all that, it's awful.'

Her pangs of torment returned, bewilderment at her
decision to put Diarmaid in the school as a boarder. Maybe
Derek O'Mahony wouldn't have killed himself otherwise.

Maybe he would.

'But the surest thing to remember,' Michael said, 'is that
all adolescents suffer terribly. I suffered terribly. So did
Diarmaid. And so did you though you mightn't realize it.
Or at least Diarmaid is suffering for you now. You're part of
his existence. He's living out a part of you.'

Her blood raced; she felt the warmth of winter cardigans
about her. No more subtle understanding had ever been put
to her, the quest of Diarmaid was one from far back in her
life, a point of suffering begun, reaching out to her son. She
loved him, she needed him, she wanted him the way she
needed the smart of an old anxiety, pain in a morning of girl-
hood when she watched sheep and thought of menstruation.

They made coffee in a silver pot.

With her back to Michael and with more certainty than
she'd ever accomplished before she asked, 'Were you and
Diarmaid lovers?'

Shock silenced the room. She turned about and he was
shaking,

'No,' he said.

She waited, poured out coffee and quietly said— as though
addressing the table-cloth. 'That's a lie.'

'It's not.'

'It is.'

Michael had the look of a stone-age man, withdrawn, wild.

'I loved Diarmaid. I didn't mean to begin what we began.
But it was mutual. Once before in his life someone tried to
seduce him. Derek at school. He'd refused point-blank. Later
the kid killed himself. The connection lasted.

Diarmaid slept with me many times. Maybe apologising in
a sense to Derek. But one night— both of us drunk on
whiskey he became hysterical and started screaming "You
queer, you. You queer, you. I don't want anything to do
with you any more," and when I tried to appease him he
started pulling at me and saying he was going home.
"Diarmaid," I said, "Go home. You'd never last a day there.

You're messed-up, and crazy. Make up your mind for once
about what you want to do. Go home, stay, go back to Alice,
but shut up.

He wept. We made love.

He woke in my arms. Like a young cripple.

Later that day we had a row. He threw jam at me. It
smattered the wall, my face. I got him, hit him.

He walked out— Michael was laughing— saying he was
going back to London to marry Alice.'

She could have cried, Susan could, but instead she felt
only tenderness and a debased sort of forgiveness for Michael.
She took him in her arms.

It was like taking Jesus. He was so quiet and slow. His
weeping ceased. She felt trouble leaving the trouble and in
the dark— faraway — she could almost hear a corncrake in
the summer-fields.

10

"Eleanor." She walked in, stampeded in. Around her arms
she'd wrapped chiffon. She looked crazy. Like a lady Susan
remembered used go to the Presbyterian church in Ballinasloe,

all sorts of shawls about her.

'Michael, I love you. Passionately.'

Michael stood there— bewildered.

'Take me, love. We'll go away. I know an ideal place. Les Saintes Maries de la Mer, gipsy capital of Europe.

Come on. We'll never get the chance again. Michael, Michael.'

Just then Susan's presence at a door-way was noticed.

'H-hello.'

'Eleanor this is Mrs O'Hallrahan, Diarmaid's mother. The mother of one of the boys in Endsleigh Gardens.'

'How do you do?'

'Hello.'

Silence. Eleanor took in the sight of a lady, middle-aged with a tan on her face and a countenance that was soft, almost pretty. Obviously she was wondering at what her presence meant.

'I came here looking for my son.'

'Your son? Here in York?'

'Yes, Eleanor. Diarmaid stayed here with me.'

Eleanor looked in bewilderment from one to the other.

'Oh.' She removed a piece of chiffon and said, 'I'm going to sit down. Darling, would you make me tea?'

Then looking at Susan, 'Are you Irish?'

'Yes.'

The 'Irish' was rolled. Like the Irish Sea.

'I come from County Galway.'

'The West?'

'Yes.'

'How wonderful.'

At that conversation ceased between them. Michael brought tea. He'd also heated buns.

They ate them with butter.

'Did you know,' Eleanor said, 'that Michael and I are getting married?'

'No.'

Susan sounded doubtful.

'Well we are. In the church in Horsham. Near where I live. It's a lovely church. Every Saturday the organ plays and couples march out. As a little girl I so wanted to get married there. Now my wish has come true. Isn't that divine?'

Her fingers clasped. Susan wasn't sure if the girl was mocking. She looked from Eleanor to Michael.

'Congratulations.'

Michael squirmed. Defeated. The look on his face said, 'O.K. I'll have to get married because Eleanor wants to get married.' That was the look. That was the way.

Susan withdrew, slept, a stranger in the house. In the morning she met Eleanor in a white night-dress emerging from Michael's room.

'Good morning.' She washed her teeth gaily. 'It's a beautiful day. Let's go shopping.'

Apparently she'd taken a fancy to Susan. It was like an indulgence to her, having the older woman in the house.

'O.K.'

They went with baskets. Eleanor picked up a bunch of lupins.

Dazzlingly she smiled.

'We'll bring these home. They'll make the house look lovely.'

11

'My father owns a lovely bungalow near Horsham. You must visit it some time. Roses all over the place. When I was small I had a pinkeen pond.

It was wonderful.' Eleanor was rhapsodizing, over lunch. Wine held in her hand. 'Remember that time we were in Paris, love, and we saw an old man paint dogs on the pavement before the police got him.' She was jumping from one thing to another, anxiously.

'I met a young man in Horsham this time who wanted to marry me. I refused. That's why I'm here. Refusals bring other decisions.'

She looked at Susan. 'Don't you agree?'

Michael was fingering a wine bottle.

'He owns a golf course.'

'Who?'

'The man who wanted to marry me.'

'Darling.' A piquant cry from Eleanor.

They went to a fair together.

More and more it seemed they were becoming more hospitable towards one another, more suited, though Susan's purpose was now totally submerged. She'd almost forgotten why she'd come. They'd forgotten why she'd come. But they were kind people and welcomed her just because she was a person, a warm person at that, and cooked good bread.

Aeroplanes turned, children ate toffee apples and candy floss. The river flowed by and ladies who'd just won teddy-bears floated excitedly about. A child cried somewhere. Eleanor turned and found a baby, a weeping little blonde baby.

The young woman raised the child. How lovely you are. Where's your mummy?'

The child's weeping subdued.

Its face began to glow, savagely, all reds, all water.

A very grumpy lady seized the child.

'I'd love to have a baby,' Eleanor said.

Turning to Susan 'she said, 'You're lucky. You have a son.'

Just then— simultaneously— they both noticed Michael. He was watching— unawares— a youth with blond hair and a chest passionately curved inwards.

Eleanor looked away, brown arms beneath a white cardigan which hung loose on her shoulders.

'Yes I'd love to have a child.'

12

They walked home. Eleanor's eyes were on the street

ahead. She was silent— looking bewildered, yet trying not to
show it. They passed shops of freshly baked scones, they
passed drifts of people, young and old. Michael was quiet,
too, unaware of problems. His forehead was somehow etched
in sun. Little paths of sun on it; it made him look both
attractive and old at once— strange, that was the word for it.
Strange.

She contemplated him, Susan did. And wondered what
would become of him. He was so shy, so nervous, so ill-at-
ease in the world. Where would he settle? Surely Eleanor
wasn't a suitable companion for him, lecturing in economics,
a suitable profession. They got home. Eleanor made lunch
automatically.

Later Susan walked into the kitchen and found her crying.

13

'Why are you crying?' It was later, another occasion. Susan
could hear their voices in the kitchen.

'I don't know why. I don't know why. I just don't know
where I'm going.'

'We're getting married, aren't we?'

'No, no— it wouldn't work.
We're not.'

There was a stunned silence.

Susan crept quietly out— past a cat— into the night.

A star hung remotely. She walked through the streets to
the cathedral where posters advertised a concert. She went in.
People looked at her, well nigh sophisticated people. She
looked sophisticated herself. Not the woman of a few months
ago; newer, more free.

In fact she wondered was it not that day when she was
driven to the station in Ballinasloe to meet Diarmaid that
she'd changed. That day he had turned up, gold and green
in the bogland.

What was she thinking of that day? Oh yes. Talking like

a madwoman about the North. Thinking of Bernadette Devlin. That day she'd changed.

She took a seat next to a gentleman with white hair.

He smiled at her.

She sat back. The young people were American. They were dressed in white. The organ began; voices reeled, songs emerging, all old ones, little understood by her.

They sang 'The Battle Hymn of the Republic.' beautifully. She was thrilled. It was so good. Why hadn't she been to a concert like this before in her life? No-one knew. Not even herself; her life was a quiet one. Now for the first time in years she felt alive.

A young man sang— as though through a vindication of her thoughts— 'There is a balm in Gilead.'

The words formed— beautifully.

Full of desire. The dead stirred. George spoke to her.

He came close, like a piece of the century, the forties, the fifties, was gone.

David Kelly, her friend from Galway, addressed her. She looked at the stained glass and remembered a time she'd gone to Mass in Galway with him at the church on the Claddagh.

'I have loved, O Lord, the beauty of Thy house and the glory which lies therein.'

Words came back from that particular Mass, Durham hills as she sped to his funeral, golds, green.

Then as never before she saw Diarmaid, hair streaked like melted butter, face half-a-girl's, looking downwards. 'Diarmaid.' The sensation was so physical she felt for a moment that he was dead, too.

Frightened by the thought she searched her mind for escape, but it scared her. Was there something wrong with him? What was the matter?

Her journey to England had not been in vain. This was it. She had to search him out. He was in danger.

This she knew. He was somewhere going wrong. She must find him.

Through the streets— walking back— an old man passed

her, raised his hat. Night had indeed fallen. Outside a chipper a girl glared into a neon-stab of light on the opposite side. A man passed.

He said 'Goodnight.' She answered politely and wondered if it would be possible, finding Diarmaid. But inside a cry arose. Firmly.

She needed to see him now.

She felt for his safety; she needed to know he was all right.

14

'Would you like a cheese sandwich?'

'Yes.'

Eleanor looked at her and prepared a sandwich.

The older woman looked wan, tired, worn-out.

'Have you been for a walk?'

'Yes.'

'Where to?'

'The cathedral.'

'How nice.'

'There was a concert on.'

'Wonderful.'

'They sang many negro spirituals and a song called 'There is a balm in Gilead.'

'I know that. I heard it in Chartres Cathedral once. I'd actually run away from home. With a boy. The gardener's assistant. He was about twenty-three. He looked just about eighteen. We went to Calais and hitched to Paris. He got fed up there and went home. Anyway he had a girl-friend at home. I went on. Beating off Moroccans and at seventeen I ended up in Chartres Cathedral for a concert. It was wonderful. A soloist sang that song and I was so moved I cried and went home.'

Silence; it was a sort of listening silence, everything awake. A dog barked outside.

Susan was quiet, ever so quiet.

'Do you like music?' Eleanor said eventually.

'Yes. Yes.'

'I'll put on a song or two.'

She put on Simon and Garfunkel.

Part of Diarmaid's repertoire, Susan thought. The two women listened— frightened. It was as though they were listening to the sound of their lives, Eleanor to her loss of Michael, Susan to her loss of Diarmaid. Eventually Eleanor said— very quietly— 'Michael went off tonight with a young boy. Somewhere they'll make love. He's not a pervert, Michael isn't; he just loves life too much.

Many people who loved life a lot were homosexuals. It's not something to worry about. I love him more. But I'll have to leave him.'

'Don't you know that people can be both homosexual and also love— be in love with women?' Susan said. In a way she was quoting an Irish woman's magazine; in another way, unbeknownst, she was quoting private experience.

'True. But he's not in love with me.'

They went to bed.

Later a door opened, Michael coming in. His footsteps sounded drunken, dazed. He put on a light and played the same L.P. that Susan and Eleanor had been listening to.

15

Her brother came for her. He was back from Cyprus, apparently, and he collected her in a black car. She kissed Michael. Then she turned to Susan and twisted her finger— with tender movement. 'Take care.'

The car drove off.

She wept later, Susan did.

She cried like a woman would for the dead long ago in Ireland.

She wept for the souls of her dead friends, for Eleanor and Michael, their failed romance.

That night they returned to the carnival grounds, Susan and Michael.

He bought a bunch of red balloons, Michael did. They were so red they looked like tomatoes. He stood beside a gully of the river and let them off.

'You should have given them to a child' Susan said.

'I don't really like children,' Michael retorted.

16

A letter from Alice, her niece.

'What in God's name are you doing in England? In York, God save us. What about your business? Come home out ot that and get some sense. You haven't fallen in love with a chimney-sweep, have you? I hope not.

Susan, darling, it's August, August, and you've been away for a long time. Your mother complains. She says I don't make corn-flakes and hot milk at night like you do. Come home, love, and start preparing for winter. People are talking. They've nothing else to say. They'll think it was in trouble you were. At your age. But you know the way it is. Where's Diarmaid? Is he in York, too? God save us. They're a desperate generation as the wireless says.

Goodbye now,
Love, Alice.

This letter was prompted by a card showing a door which Susan had sent to Ireland— rather unwisely— bearing her York address. She took it as a rebuff, Susan did. What business was it of theirs?

Scorched she searched for solace. She went out, walked, attended a fashion show. She was after all having the time of her life— or was she? Was it not time to go now? Had she not made this decision? That Diarmaid was in need of her, that she was going to him because like a trapeze artist he was flying on a very high tight-rope.

He was getting drunk a lot now, Michael was, and her mind

was wandering. She felt this now. Was she going batty? Putting on lipstick— Eleanor had given her the shade— dressing up, walking among ladies with their poodles.

She'd watched Michael but that was it. He was drinking whiskey. She watched as though he were a very audacious child but like some very solid matron having given up hope of change. They looked at one another often with the look of inmates.

Then one night she got drunk. On brandy. The wallpaper pink she shoved thoughts of going to Diarmaid out of her mind. Lately she'd been thinking of it, she'd been wanting it, but knowing she couldn't move. This house stuck to her. Like a pillow. She just felt like going on and on here. There was nothing else to do. Michael was slobbering now.

'Shut up,' she said to him.

She was surprised at her own vindictiveness.

'Fuck off,' he said to her. 'Fuck off, you old hag.' Then he looked at her laughing. 'Come to me.' He put his arms about her.

'You're the loveliest person I've met.'

She stroked his hair; her palm felt his skull.

'Darling.'

She wove her hands through his hair.

'You're tired,' she said to him. 'You're very tired. You need a rest.

You need to be away from England. You should take a holiday. Put your troubles aside.

Leave them alone. They'll go away.'

'They won't.' He was weeping.

'Yes, love, they will. They will.'

She woke up some hours later. She'd actually slept beside him. There he was, head on a cushion.

She got up, steadied herself. Lord Jesus. What would everyone say? With some delight at the idea that she'd slept alongside a man half her age, she rose.

Then looking at Michael she realized it wasn't so much a man she'd slept beside as a child.

She fetched a rug, put it over him.

And quietly— in a way she'd not forget— went to bed.

17

'I'm going to London. I feel I must see Diarmaid.'

Michael looked at her.

'You'll find he's changed.'

'No.'

'Yes. For one thing he's cut his hair; he looks older. In fact he's quite a person now. And a bit less guileless than he was. In fact he'd cut your throat in a minute.'

'What do you mean?'

'Diarmaid is now a young man.'

She tried to picture him with his hair cut again, but couldn't.

'Listen. I've had enough. I know I must see him. I came here to see him. I'll go to see him.'

'O.K. Go.'

Michael left the room. He came back in a minute.

'You won't have anything to say to him, he's changed so much.'

When Michael had gone to visit a university colleague Susan wept and wept.

He'd been so cruel, so cruel. She waited, listened. For the first time in her life she thought of suicide. 'O God.

She wanted to die.

18

They drank again that night.

'You've been betrayed by age,' Michael told her. 'People like you shouldn't grow old.'

She was beginning to hate him.

'You loved your son. You poured love on him, but now

look at him, crazy, mixed-up.

For God's sake, woman, wake up. You and your son, it's over. You can't live in your womb all your life. Live in some-one else's.' And he laughed, bitterly, cruelly. 'I hurt him,' he then said. To himself. She thought he was going a bit crazy.

It was three o' clock. He was wearing a baineen sweater.

'Did you know? He tried to kill himself. That's why he left.'

'No. Why? Where?'

'It was too much for him— the sin, the sex. He was totally confused.

He called me a pervert one day. I said nothing. Then replied he was as much involved as I. Besides I told him he was a twit. He needed me. He cared for me. More than his bloody mother or Derek O'Mahony. Someone like Derek had only clung to him because he was sympathetic. Derek was a savage, too. He'd drained part of Diarmaid.

Then one night— we had a fight— Diarmaid slit his wrists. Peculiar, isn't it? And wailed "I want to get out." '

'Out of where?' Susan questioned urgently.

'Hell.'

'But Diarmaid, Diarmaid,' Susan said, 'was in Heaven. He was happy just waiting for trains or buying records in Ballinasloe. He was simple. Like his father. I don't care what you say.'

Diarmaid. Diarmaid. Diarmaid. Who was he anyway? His reality had failed. Her son had fled. And suddenly she saw him— in a white jersey like Michael's— totally before her, streaks of blond through his hair. He was her son, a boy, and also her closest relationship. She must go to him now, immediately. He'd tried to die because it wasn't happening any more, the intensity.

It was over, marsh-land football pitches, packets of cigarettes in the wind. And a song called 'Ruby Tuesday.'

He was a man without his adolescence now. He was a human failure.

'No. Diarmaid wasn't just happy waiting for trains. He's

not that simple. He's complicated. Like the rest of us he wouldn't give up his childhood dream. Now look at him. Off with a girl somewhere, another misfit.' Michael went on and on. 'Everything was black and white to him once.

He'd borne a grudge— well. Against school, against life, against those who'd driven Derek O'Mahony to kill himself. They were evil. But in his relationship with me he found good and bad— mainly bad.

He found— among the bed-sheets— evil in himself. That he couldn't understand or take. He'd always wanted to believe himself an angel. You'd helped complete the picture. But it didn't work out. It broke. He broke with it.'

Michael's eyes were red, 'red as roses', Susan thought, and it occurred to her how frigid her language and thoughts had become, like poetry, a distance between them and life. Where had she strayed? To a picture like Diarmaid's ikons, to a way of life which substituted art for life.

Here she was, make-up on, discussing her son as though he were a plaything. It was so wrong. She had to find him now, hug him to her, make him real.

'He's cut his hair now.' The phrase rang. Yes, he'd cut his hair. He was different, adult. All that was intense and problematic was probably gone. But what remained was what she wanted to meet, an adult child, someone she wanted simply to say 'Hello' to.

19

She left early in the afternoon. She'd delayed because they'd made a big breakfast, threw everything into the pan, apples, ham, eggs, radishes, tomatoes, onions, remorseless scallions.

It was hard to divorce yourself from a way of life which made you a queen, an empress, an undefeated exponent of art, of country, of culture. There in York she'd been accepted as a sort of Celtic demi-goddess, and she'd known how to play up to people's wiles.

It was late in the afternoon when the train reached the Midlands and within a few hours it was dark.

It was a cold, lonely dark which seemed to hold the ghost of Diarmaid crying last Easter. It was a different Diarmaid that existed now. 'More's the pity,' Susan said.

The train flew in past London suburbs, lighted houses. In any of these she and George could have made love during the war years. She felt an acute desperation. She'd never really lived up to George's expectation of her. He'd always fled her, that was why. She'd been too calm, too timid and half-in-love with a grocer's assistant.

A woman on the train handed her an Evangelist prayer. Susan took it. The woman sped off. At the station danger encroached. Susan knew. There in the dark a cripple stood selling wilted flowers. She brushed past but it was as though his eyes said, 'I know. I know all about it, your foolish life.'

She took a bus to Ladbroke Grove. There Bridget greeted her.

'Susan. Holy Mary, I'm cured. I'm cured.'

And Susan kissed, hugging her, as though it were she herself who was cured.

20

On Sunday they went to Mass in Westminster Cathedral. The Mass was sung. They received Holy Communion. Later they joined hands coming out of the church.

21

Such was their joy that they went to Battersea Fun-fair. There they bought ice-cream and behaved like children. The Thames flowed nearby. There were lights on Chelsea bridge and Susan felt like wading towards them. It was all strange

115

in her head now. Bridget's cure had totally submerged her need for Diarmaid. These days were days of thanksgiving for a human failure.

22

She thought she saw him. Through the lights. Holding a girl's hand. She ran. Speed picked him. Was it him? His hair was dark, blindly dark. Yet blond in it.

She called. Then realized it wasn't him. He'd cut his hair anyway and this boy had long streaks of dark hair.

'Last night as I lay on my pillow,
Last night as I lay on my bed,
Last night as I lay on my pillow,
I dreamt that my Bonnie was dead.'

Bridget was singing, combing her hair which was grey.

'I was wondering what I'll do now that I'm to live. I'd planned for death.'

'Take a holiday.'

Susan seemed to be telling this to everyone now that her own holiday had succeeded so well.

'Yes. That's what I'll do. I'll go back to Ireland. The green fields. Thanks be to God for these and to His Blessed Mother. Thanks be to God for life.'

23

Walking down a street she thought she saw him in a bus. This time his hair was short. The bus was an ordinary red one, but it looked like a weapon. Why was that? Perhaps because it reminded her she was in England and buses didn't look like that in Ireland. She was in a strange country. Why? Basically in search of re-assurance.

For once and for all she had to see Diarmaid now and go.

Alice answered the door. She drew back from the sight of Susan.

'H-hello.'

And then 'Come in.' The room inside looked like the aftermath of a bad party. Cups thrown about, sugar sticking to spoons.

'How are you?'

'O.K. And you?'

'Fine.'

'You're looking absolutely excellent. You're not like a mother at all. You look like someone's – '

She didn't finish the sentence. She looked rather distracted.

'S– sit down.'

The girl looked into the older woman's eyes. Her own eyes blue. And Susan thought her skin looked like the colour of woodbine.

'Are you O.K. love?'

She began to cry, the girl did.

She wept with total abandon, then looked at Susan.

'He's gone.'

'Gone where?'

'I don't know. He's so different. Ever since he went to York, he swears and curses.

He's living with some Irish guys now who go on speaking about the Provisional I.R.A. and bombings as though it were fun and admirable.

He curses, swears, fucks.'

It took something to say the last word, but it was the only one the girl could have honestly used.

'He beat me up one night because I wouldn't make love to him. He's gone round the bend.'

Susan listened, glued to the armchair.

She couldn't speak, couldn't move.

'That's terrible,' was all she could say. 'That's terrible.'

In Piccadilly Circus she wept until the tears ceased coming.

No-one looked at her though at one stage a Salvation Army lady threatened to approach.

She wept until she could see no-one and finally had to walk on without tears. It's far from Galway, she said to herself. At least if she went home there'd be green fields and the sound of birds and the quiet of old people's faces.

Even if death were more imminent than ever. Her own death.

For there was nothing left now but the slow trudge to the grave.

26

On Sunday she went to Trafalgar Square with Bridget. There they were able to view an Irish march against internment. Posters held up. 'Give us back our sons.' 'Death to the traitors.' They frightened her, the posters. Especially the ones bearing notes of vengeance. And she felt bitterness against these people. They'd taken her son. Would he be blowing up bridges soon or damaging the faces of innocent children? She hoped not. Yet as she looked she could only feel sorrow for the marchers. Internment indeed was a terrible thing, but vengeance impossible. No-one had the right to vengeance, no-one could take over God's power. These women with their hardened faces would have to step back.

They couldn't kill, kill and keep on killing.

Murder was stupid. Murder was remorseless, murder was evil.

Walking away the voice of a Derry woman shouting from the crowd haunted her.

'They've taken our homes, sons, husbands, families. They'll never take our dignity.'

And she wondered what dignity was in smouldering fires, and bombs waiting at shop-doors.

Yet she realized it was their problem, not hers.

She couldn't comment, she couldn't cope with it. All she knew was that her own son was among the ranks of these people now.

27

Bridget took a few days off work so she stayed on to accompany her about London. They visited Christopher Wren's church in Piccadilly; they visited many Wimpy bars and some more staid coffee shops. They even went to a ballet, 'Giselle.'

They were lovely days; September weighed heavily inside Susan. It was Autumn and days strolled by like polite children in the parks. It was time to go. Gradually, uneasily she packed. Then one day from a bus she definitely saw Diarmaid. Looking rather lost. She got off and searched for him. There was no sign of him.

She looked all over Oxford Street until rather bedraggled she arrived in a coffee shop and started to cry.

'What's wrong, dear?'

An old lady approached her.

Susan looked at her.

'I came to England searching for my son,' she said in a strong West of Ireland accent, 'and I can't find him.'

'Listen, love. I'm sure there's a way.'

The woman might have been from the North; she had a Yorkshire accent.

'First he was a hippie; now he's a member of the I.R.A.'

Susan spoke like any grief-stricken Irish-woman.

'It's a phase, love. It's a phase.

My own son was in jail for rape.'

Susan looked at her— almost frightened.

She took the other woman's hand.

'I know the country you come from. It's beautiful.' Susan was talking of Durham and Yorkshire, land that was lovely, but populated with bizarre factories.

This time it was Susan who had the voice of comfort.

'Young lads can be driven to desperate things when the lives they're leading are unfair. It's unfair to put a child in a school where he'll be caned. It's unfair to put a child in a factory where he'll lose his soul.'

The other woman clutched her fingers. 'How true. I never thought of it like that.

My son has been working in a factory since he was sixteen. I shouldn't have done that to him. He deserved more. He always loved painting. I think he's keen on being an artist.'

'Give him the chance.'

'And your son?'

'He doesn't know what he wants to be. He paints, too. Or rather he makes little collages. You know, putting bits and pieces of things together.'

The woman from the North was fascinated.

'They're not far apart then, are they?'

'No.'

'Why don't you go and look for your son now? Make a big effort and you'll find him. Crying will get you nowhere.'

Susan looked at her with gratitude and dried her eyes with a handkerchief bearing a message from Our Lady of Knock on one of its borders.

'I'll do that,' she said.

Later that day with words of comfort ringing in her ears she returned to Endsleigh Gardens.

There she approached Alice who'd just come in from selling a pamphlet, a shoulder bag hanging from her.

It had never occurred to her to ask Alice if she knew where Diarmaid was living now.

'Yes, he's in Harrow. I'll get his address.'

Susan sat down. A boy came in and played a guitar. The music was soothing, calming; the boy wore a white shirt with pink embroidery.

They didn't say anything to one another.

The boy played with love in his music and Susan was grateful for having heard him.

28

She went to Mass before going to see Diarmaid. It was as
though she were preparing for an extraordinary event. Half
way through the Mass— she'd been drinking port wine with
Bridget the previous night— she realized she was attending a
Jewish ceremony.

It hadn't even occurred to her to look at what was going
on Hedonism had gripped her that hard.

She sought the entrance but a Jewish boy smiled at her so
benevolently that she stayed.

29

Across a bridge in Harrow she went. Underneath trains
passed. The day was passionately grey. She'd plucked a rose
from a bush and she threw it into the air.

People passed, looked.

The dramatics over she went on, feeling more at peace
than she'd ever felt before.

30

She met a man who asked directions of her. Naturally she
couldn't give them, but instead they spoke about the weather.

He was Irish; in a moment he was launching into names.
Did she know so-and-so? He came from quite near her.

She knew or didn't wish to know anybody.

She turned. This was the road leading towards Diarmaid's
house.

31

And then— like a huge sensation— she passed a grave-yard.

121

What was it? Why was it? She remembered something. A grave-yard in Harrow, a boy she'd known in Galway buried here.

She entered.

Sure enough after an hour of searching she found it.

David Kelly, Died 1942, Durham.

Native of Kilconnell, Co. Galway.

May God have mercy on his soul.

She knelt and tasted the earth with her mouth. It was like tasting another woman's nipple or the sexual organ of a man.

She leant and tasted life.

For this was it, what her life was. It could be no more, a love relationship with a boy— George— her husband. For that's what he'd always be, a boy. Then a sneaking glimpsory relationship with another boy, David Kelly, grocer's assistant, a boy she's actually gone to a Joan Crawford film with once while her husband-to-be was in Athenry. Nothing had ever come of it but they'd loved one another passionately. His destiny as a gardener in Durham was her destiny. His death, her death, the death of a dream. And on top of that, both of them, was Diarmaid like a sum. George, David, Diarmaid, the summation of her life, the three people she'd really loved, openly, defiantly.

She stood weeping. Tears flowed. Her whole being became like a tidal wave.

Here now it was over.

Whatever would happen had already ceased to happen. Life couldn't go on beyond this point.

They were locked in a dream, Diarmaid, David, George, all heads together, locked into a misfit spirit.

Before she departed from David's grave she left a prayer as she'd been taught to do as a child and wandered away, other figures retreating, women in black stockings, mourning their dead.

122

32

A girl answered the door. She had a wiry, unwholesome face and she was dressed mainly in black.

'Hello.' Her lips, thin, hardly seemed to open.

'How are you? Do you know Diarmaid O'Hallrahan?'

'Yes. Are you a relation? His mother?'

'Yes.'

'Come in.'

Susan entered.

Inside the hallway was bleak.

It was dark and brown and very, very unhealthy looking. The girl showed her into a room.

And immediately Susan was reminded of the Men's Social Club in Ballinasloe except that here hung a picture of Patrick Pearse and the Republican colours.

Under Pearse was an array of pictures of people regarded as criminals by English newspapers, regarded as heroes among certain sectors in Ireland.

In pubs, in schools, in the mouth-pieces of the Republican movement, columns in Irish newspapers.

'Sit yourself down. I'll make tea.' Susan was immediately struck by the quietness of the girl.

She didn't dare open her mouth. The girl moved like a very betrayed virgin.

Her movements were quiet, shielded, pathetic almost.

While sitting there Susan was sure she heard a baby's squeal somewhere. Then maybe the tight little scratching of a mouse.

'I hope you didn't come here hoping to see Diarmaid,' the girl said almost in a murmuring voice.

'Why? Is he gone?'

'He left yesterday.'

Susan was amazed. For one moment she thought it might be back to Ireland he was gone. She thrilled, delighted.

Maybe he was going to University College, Galway, after all.

'He left with a young man, a very weird young man, for Yugoslavia.'

'What?'

'Some friend of his. I forget his name.

You see Diarmaid had been staying here for a while; he'd often looked after the baby and Tommy was very fond of him. Tommy is my husband.

They weren't militant republicans as the papers say.

I suppose just both of them believed in a cause.'

'A cause?'

'Yes, Ireland. You see Tommy is from Derry and–' with peculiar viciousness to the older woman she said–, he had his balls cut off by the British army.'

Susan smarted; the woman was sorry. She seemed to withdraw part of the statement.

'He's fine now. He's got over it– maybe physically he's adjusted, but you can't get over it mentally.

You can't forget. You can't forget what they're doing to your houses, your families, your children. Can you put torture, murder, humiliation out of mind?

I love Derry but we couldn't get a house there. Anyway after Tommy was interned no-one wished to know us. Even a lot of Catholics, bloody cowards. We came here.

Tommy got a job but the rest of his life he'll dedicate himself to the freedom of Ireland.'

'How?'

The girl looked quizzical.

'By serving the Republican movement.

There's no other way.'

'With bombs?'

Susan was unsure of her footing but she knew in herself what was wrong and hysterical.

'Yes if we have to.'

'Did Diarmaid– subscribe to these beliefs?'

Susan felt like an inspector.

'For a while. For a while.'

'And what happened?'

The baby was crying.

She went in and fetched it.

'This guy came and collected him.

Some friend of his from the North.

He wasn't bad but God knows it looks a bit funny a young guy going off with a fellow like that to Yugoslavia.'

'What did he look like?'

Susan got a description of Michael. Anyway she hadn't really needed to ask.

A grim toll was taken.

She couldn't believe that Diarmaid had gone off to Yugoslavia with Michael.

She couldn't understand it.

She listened.

'The trouble started when Tommy and I weren't getting on too well.

Diarmaid came then. Tommy had met him in a pub.

He was in need of a home.

He looked starved. But also he was in need of friends.

Tommy took an immediate liking to him.

He liked the look of the fellow, the sincerity.

They drank, joked, talked about politics together.

But what neither of them understood was that I was lonely and when Diarmaid began to talk a lot to me Tommy became jealous. You know the way.

One night in a pub Tommy slashed a bottle of Guinness over Diarmaid's head.

I think it was afterwards Diarmaid wrote to his friend in the North and then they telephoned one another and arranged to go away together. It sounds peculiar, doesn't it, live, young men going away together.'

Susan was shattered.

Quietly the other woman withdrew. She was making lunch. 'Tommy will be home soon,' she said. It suddenly occurred to Susan that she didn't want to meet Tommy and she left, saying she had to meet some people.

33

It was almost incredible. Had they really gone away? To Yugoslavia. Was it on holiday or to live? Both of them together again. What had come into Diarmaid? Had he realized the Republican movement wasn't really him and he had to go back, not to gentle Diarmaid of before, but to his relationship with Michael.

Two young men with strange faces, they suited one another.

She got a bus. A Jewish funeral pulled about Golder's Green. A lady in black led the mourners. All around the hearse were garlands of flowers, reds and blues and greens.

She wanted to know, quietly, desperately, Michael and Diarmaid were both part of her now. Had Michael gone behind her back and taken Diarmaid on the last league of the journey, abducted him to sin, to sodomy?

What was it? Why was it?

'Susan, Diarmaid was here,' Bridget said when she got home.

'What?'

'He called for a jumper.'

'Where is he now?'

'Gone to Yugoslavia. There was a young man with him. They were both going to live there, they said. The young man apparently got hold of a house together.'

'Did you tell him I was here?'

'Yes. But they were in a hurry. They had to catch a ferry to Ostend.'

'They didn't wait?'

'They were in a hurry.'

'But Diarmaid.'

Bridget took her arm.

'Your son has changed, Susan.'

'Diarmaid.'

'Listen, love.'

Susan wept, she wept openly on the floor.

'The young man with him said he knows you.
He told me to give you his regards.'

34

He'd left behind a jumper in Bridget's apartment. He'd
called for it, a white jumper.
Susan singled out her clothes, preparing to go home. She
found a white jumper of her own. She tossed it on the floor.
She didn't wish for any reminders.

35

'He was wearing a crew-neck shirt,' Bridget said, describing
Michael— though Susan didn't want to hear.
She was left astonished by the whole business, she wanted
to forget. Though Bridget, pressed on by something, made it
seem that the Mafia had called at her door-step.
She hadn't an idea why Michael and Diarmaid had gone off
together, they could be going on a boys' outing for all she
knew. But to Susan it was blatantly, obviously clear.
They'd gone. they'd deserted her because she was old and
unbeautiful.
They'd gone in the stride and the eternal cruelty of youth,
In the fullest sense both were traitors.

36

She thought of it that night.
Outside the lights looked like skeletons.
All their heads like skulls.
People passed; the curtains were fraught with wind.
He'd gone, he'd left because he was rejecting, rejecting all.
And his rejection had led to hatred, hatred of his home, his

mother, the gentleness she's brought on him, the loveliness of vision, of life.

Long ago Ireland had mangled him, twisted him, embittered him.

Now his mother embittered him because she'd made him quiet and loving.

He'd gone towards the I.R.A. to tear out the terribleness of loving, the niceties of behaviour and the warmth, the humours of a country kitchen his mother had imposed on him.

And when it hadn't worked— the I.R.A.— he'd gone back to another sort of rejection, this time adapting it not only to reject Ireland and the people who'd driven Derek O'Mahony to murder, but to reject his mother, her veniality, her sympathy with him.

He didn't want her sympathy; it was clear and ugly now. He didn't want her love. He didn't want her.

37

'When I find myself in times of trouble.
Mother Mary comforts me,
Bearing words of wisdom,
Let it be. Let it be.'
The radio was blaring when Susan was eating her breakfast in the morning.

But the music was pleasant and the words calm.

'I'll miss you,' Bridget said as she decapitated an egg.

'On Sundays I'll pray for you.'

Susan was comforted by the words.

Before breakfast was finished though, Susan asked,

'Didn't Diarmaid say anything before he left?'

'Yes, yes. He was asking for you.'

But something of fatality overcame Bridget's reply and Susan kept silent. He hadn't even waited to say goodbye.

38

Trains whistled, Euston was crowded.

As Bridget stood before her images ran through Susan's brain, the time both Diarmaid and Derek played girls in a school play, a hangman's tree.

'Goodbye, love. You've brought me great luck.'

Bridget's kiss was wet.

Susan cried.

'Goodbye, love. Goodbye.

I must rush.

Goodbye.'

War, blitz, these are the things she thought of. The September night was dark; London sped by.

This was probably the last time she'd see the city where she welcomed George's arms after the war. She sat back in her seat, frozen.

After a while she noticed a woman opposite her.

'Hello.'

She vaguely recognised the smile.

Yes, it was Miss Hanratty, a teacher from Ballinasloe.

'How are you? I know you but I can't place you.'

'I'm Susan O'Hallrahan.'

'Yes, yes. You're a dress-maker. I see your little shop on the Galway Road.

I've seen you in passing on the way to Galway. I was doing a B.A. by night there last year and I'd often spy you.

With your son it must have been.'

'Diarmaid.'

The woman smiled broadly.

She had on a pink dress. she looked tanned, healthy, but inevitably aged.

'I've just been in Italy,' she announced.

'In Trieste.

And in Venice. Oh, it was gorgeous.'

'How lovely,' Susan said, all of a sudden very English.

'It was beautiful. I was saving so long for a holiday like this. Now I've got my way. I can still hear it,' she said, arms in the air, 'the chorus of Aida echoing down the Grand Canal.'

41

Liverpool vacated the shelves of her mind, all the lights, all the boats, a deeply depressed sort of beauty about them.

She was going back to Ireland. But not as a country-woman.

For years she'd camouflaged herself as one, but the last weeks had shown one thing; she was capable of being accepted by any culture. She was a woman of intelligence and beauty, and if she'd spent her life listening to curlews and watching the rainbow-side of the sky it was because all the time, inside, she was performing her own private part in history, rejecting Ireland, the evil of conformity by outwardly accepting it, but inside taking on George's body against hers on a starry night in 1939.

She was without shame. She'd given birth. She'd loved her son. He'd gone from her now, indeed far from the land, but always inside he'd wear the camouflage inside him, behind the barrier of social rejection, of casting off society, he'd wear a very private idea of love, an idea amounting to teddy-bears when he was two and the grey ikons he created at seventeen.

'Susan.'
Miss Hanratty was calling.
'Come in. It's raining.
Look what I've found.'
She produced a bottle of wine.
'An Italian friend made it.'
The colour was yellow, homely.
'Let's drink it,' she said.
Her nose ran with rain.
She sat down, Susan did.
Miss Hanratty had on a rain-coat.
They sat close and drank the wine.
In the morning— as the boat entered the North Wall—
they woke to find their bodies lying on top of one another.

EPILOGUE

1

The priest had an affair with a young girl that Autumn.
The whole parish knew. She was bundled off, pregnant, to a
convent near Dublin where she'd wash dirty linen before
having her offspring.

So therefore aspects changed and people gossiped less, a
whole conviction gone astray, the Christ in the church
looking rather numb and insane on the cross.

They watched 'Ironside' instead, television cops and
robber games, and more then one woman had to take
sedation in Ballinasloe mental hospital.

2

Mrs O'Hallrahan returned like Joseph from Egypt, re-
instated in her dress-making shop, no-one supposing anything, leaving her aside.

3

'Good morning, Mrs O'Hallrahan,'
The parson called one morning.
'How are you?'
'Fine. Grand, thanks.'
'You're looking well tanned after your holiday.'
'You're grand yourself.'
'Thanks. I was in County Wexford. Beside the sea.'
'Gorgeous.'
'You were in York, I believe.'
'Yes. I was there once. Long ago.'
'It's a beautiful town.'
Susan smiled. 'I loved it.'

'What I came to ask you was would you make a dress for my daughter. She's becoming engaged.'

'Oh that's wonderful.'

'To a young man from Bristol,' the parson said before she asked. 'They met at a party in Dublin.'

On and on it went, the parties and the garden parties, the whole Church of Ireland ethic, Protestantism sinking with a grubby face.

'I hope they're happy,' Susan said.

'Soon your own son may be thinking of marriage. It's surprising how early they wed these days.'

'He might well do that.'

Susan's smile was a damaged one, but it was not too unhappy.

She liked talking to the old man. No matter what he said.

'I'd be delighted to make a dress for your daughter.'

'You've got her measurements?'

'Yes.'

'And do you know— she's leaving the material to your discretion!'

Susan smiled.

It was a compliment.

On and on the conversation went until she invited him into tea and could observe his old Protestant face against the profane colours of a Sacred Heart picture.

·4

'How's Diarmaid?'

Mrs Conlon touched her arm in the pub one night.

'Grand.'

Susan jumped slightly.

Mrs Conlon smiled knowingly.

'That's good.'

5

She wondered why he didn't write. Was he that begrudging? And again she wondered at his sullenness.

Obviously he'd found himself betrayed by everything she taught him. Gentleness didn't match up to life, one was betrayed, one betrayed others.

He probably felt he'd betrayed Derek O'Mahony.

Perhaps he felt she hadn't really cared for him but had coaxed him into a state where his whole mind was numb and unaware.

Thinking like this her face seemed to harden, become bitter, sad, remorseful.

But she fled the mirror like an enemy until one morning in the hallway mirror she glimpsed a card that showed blue sky.

'Hello. Sorry for not writing before. It's lovely here. We live beside the sea. It's blue. All the time and the people are lovely. We catch fish. Even in winter.

It feels miles from Galway here.

Michael sends love. Look after yourself.
Always,
Diarmaid'

The 'always' got her. 'Always' what? Always nothing. She felt like cursing him. It was like a slight, just a casual slight.

There wasn't depth, there wasn't love in it.

She crumbled the card and was about to put it in the fire when on second thoughts she read it over again and wept.

6

The women's organization flourished.

Susan headed off to tinker encampments with them where she fed young children on tinned sweets.

The idea was unwise she often thought.

'Would you like to mind this little boy for a while?' Mrs

Keating asked her one day. A boy whose mother had died and was awaiting an aunt in England.

He wasn't really a child, about fifteen.

Susan— out of the goodness of her heart she thought at the time— brought him home.

He ate corn-flakes with her at night.

'What's your ambition in life, Mickey?'

'What's ambition?'

'What do you hope to do?'

'Become a pilot.'

The usual answer.

'Why?'

'Because I'd like to see the rhinoceroses.'

'What?'

'The big things you see in the pictures.'

'But you don't have to be a pilot to see them.'

'Mammy said you had.'

And Susan realized his Mammy was dead.

'She's right I think.'

After twelve that night Susan caught Mickey sneaking out the back-door with a silver table-set under his arm in a big box.

'Where are you going?'

He dropped the box and made off. She never saw him again.

Mrs Keating laughed.

The ladies chuckled.

It was one of those incidents which saved her from going mad.

7

A letter came. She devoured its contents.

'Mammy,

It's getting cold here but it's still very beautiful. We went on a trip to Venice. It was lovely though it rained a lot. I'll never forget travelling at night up the Grand Canal.

I thought how you'd really love it. The tourists are gone. We have San Marco's Square to ourselves. They say the city is sinking. You can feel it.

In a cafe where men were playing billiards I thought of you.

How are you? Would you like to visit us at Christmas? There are three American girls staying here. They're a bit silly but I think you'd like them. You could get a plane to Dubrovnik and then get a train here. Michael's writing a play. An earlier one he wrote has been accepted by the B.B.C. So I don't think he's going back to college. It's very nice here. At the moment the sun is setting and all around us is an immense glow.

You can almost smell fish in the twilight.

Please write soon,

Love,

Diarmaid.'

Susan carefully considered the contents.

And then wrote back to say she couldn't come.

As she posted the letter in a green box a snowflake touched her finger-nail.

8

After that there were no letters. The silence lasted over Christmas. It was the loneliest Christmas of her life— mummers went by on Saint Stephen's Day, calling out their traditional tunes, 'A penny for the wren. A penny for the wren.' They wore traditional costumes, old pajama tops and lipstick.

She gave them scones.

Around them East Galway was lit up, the land delved, mountains, distant, were soft.

She'd never felt closer to God, to eternity, to the eternal hue of life that poets must have written about, all that was good and mature in life.

She prayed over the infant in the local crib.

Mrs Conlon had given her a plant for Christmas and she placed it alongside a candle, a traditional Irish act of love, a candle at a window at Christmas to guide stray dogs and angels.

9

Towards the New Year a multitude of young people passed, hitch-hikers from Dublin, from London, going West. They hitched outside her door.

One day she noticed a young pair standing for hours.

She went to the door.

'Hello, out there. Would you like a cup of tea?'

'We'd love one, thanks.'

They were from Birmingham, both going to art school.

She sat them down.

And made tea, cutting enormous slices of Christmas cake for them.

They were glad of her company as she was of theirs.

The girl had blonde hair, was wrapped in an anorak.

About her neck was a blue and white scarf.

'Who made the ikon?'

Susan was glad she called it an ikon, too.

'My son.'

'Your son? Is he in art school, too?'

'No. He lives in Yugoslavia.'

'Oh.'

The girl gazed, fascinated.

The ikon was of a girl with linen-coloured hair— he'd used bits of linen, Diarmaid had, to make the hair.

The girl looked out, a blazing Madonna, the one in the ikon, her eyes bright, bead-like.

'It's very unusual,' the English girl said, 'half-way between a Russian ikon and a collage some child would make. It's

138

very, very beautiful.

It really seems to say something.'

No, it's just a girl, Susan thought, just a girl. But constructed as mediaeval ikons were, to explain a myth.

Susan glimpsed herself in the mirror as she spoke to the young people.

She hadn't realized it.

She'd grown old and drab, grey hair falling, without sparkle.

She looked like any other Irishwoman, aging ceaselessly, without hope, interest or spectacle left in her life.

'I hope your son keeps on going with art,' the girl said.

'He'll keep on going anyway,' Susan smiled, 'All you young people do.'

She bade them farewell. They got a lift immediately. She watched the landscape take them over in the little car.

10

At nights she watched television now in Mrs Conlon's pub, 'Ironside,' dreadful American programmes. She drank Guinness and listened to the stories of old men when there were plays on the television and no-one was interested.

One night the whole pub watched with fascination as the act of love was shown on the screen.

'Dirt,' someone murmured, but most watched in awe.

Someone in the pub must have realized it was no more unwholesome than watching sparrows mate, for the feeling afterwards was one of calm.

11

Often now Susan took a break from work and sat in the pub during the day.

If Mrs Conlon was busy she'd sit alone. It was veering

towards February and she found herself watching the road West as she had been doing a year previously, taking in the road to the Estoria in Galway where she saw Joan Crawford in 1939 and kissed George for the first time.

On bright days she stood outside her door and remembered ladies in scarlet and black in 1938, Galway, boats to Aran, picnics on the beach in Spiddal and nuns who bathed on private beaches.

12

On February 28th. Mrs Conlon died.

Her funeral was in March. Sleet fell, many mourned, her pub bore black ribbons.

'Requiescat in pace.'

Susan wept louder than anybody.

She bent and touched the grave with her fingers. Sleet became drizzle; the priest read the prayers. Everyone realized a local gossip had passed away, and Susan knew that it was over, the solicitude of a pub and a pint of Guinness.

13

'Good morning, Mrs O'Hallrahan.'

The parson called.

'Could you make my daughter's wedding dress?'

'That would be lovely.'

'She'd like a blue one. She's very attracted to the colour blue.'

'I am, too,' Susan said. 'It's a very nostalgic colour.'

'That's it,' said the parson. 'Nostalgic. It reminds one of cups of tea in a garden long ago when the days seemed much warmer.'

'It reminds me of sorrow,' Susan said.

'What do you mean?'

'In the Catholic Church it's the Virgin Mary's colour, and she if anyone suffered a great deal.'

'Come now, Mrs O'Hallrahan, you can't discriminate. There's great devotion to Mary in the Church of Ireland.'

'But your Mary is white. Ours is blue. I don't mean 'ours' in a bigoted sense. I mean in the way you visited churches when you were very small and saw dream-like Blessed Virgins with candles lighting before them. And for me in the small church the blue of the Virgin Mary was the blue of Ireland, the blue of famine and thirst and the terrible ghost stories old ladies would tell.'

The parson was suitably impressed.

'Indeed you're right. But I'm sure for Eleanor it's a different motif. She probably likes blue because it's fashionable.'

'That's right. I'll buy material in Cullen's in Ballinasloe. I wonder could she come in and help me.'

'I hope so.'

'O.K.'

Just then the doctor's wife came.

'Mrs O'Hallrahan could you make a summer frock for me? I'm going to Yugoslavia for a Spring holiday.'

And Susan could only smile, bitterly, silently to herself.

14

In time people ceased asking questions.

They didn't want to know anymore now.

The idea of a boy in an anorak with a Rolling Stones album under his arm which was once revolutionary was now old-hat.

They didn't need to know about Diarmaid.

Most knew he didn't write, and if he wrote it was very infrequently, so with time, as Susan's spirit grew bleaker and her hair greyer, she became among the fields, the houses, and the lack of Guinness bottles, just another local tragedy.

Other Fiction
from Writers and Readers

A Painter of our Time
by John Berger

Janos Lavin is a refugee from pre-war Hungary. A week after the opening of his first London exhibition, Lavin vanishes from the city he has lived in for the last twenty years. Why?

Through a diary whose urgency and insight are reminiscent of Van Gogh's letters and Gauguin's diaries, Berger records Lavin's preoccupations and his mounting inner conflict as the Hungarian revolutionary crisis of 1956 approaches.

In this, his first novel, John Berger raises important questions about the artist's place in society, and the relationship between art and revolutionary politics.

"Berger . . . keeps on asking difficult public questions at a time when few English novelists worry about anything other than the private ones." C.J. Driver *The Guardian*

"The many-layered view of people and situations . . . gives Berger his powerful density." Marie Peel *The Tribune*

ISBN 0 904613 13 5

Reasons of State
by Alejo Carpentier
translated by Francis Partridge

Subtle, savage, intoxicating, *Reasons of State* tells
the story of a Latin American dictator who is repeatedly
forced to leave the pleasures of Paris life to put down
rebellions at home. Carpentier's understanding of the
psychology of power, his depiction of life and politics
in a third world nation, are unmatched.

Reasons of State has been translated into eight
languages and acclaimed everywhere. It has been made
into a film to be premiered at the 1978 Cannes Film
Festival.

"This is an immense and generous book; immense in
its conception and penetration of the ruthless mechanics
of power, generous in its characterisation and breadth of
vision." Peter Tinniswood *The Times*

"The writing makes a continually intoxicating
bravura, giddying with imaginative inventiveness."
Valentine Cunningham *New Statesman*

ISBN 0 904613 52 6

The Writers and Readers Publishing Cooperative

was formed in the autumn of 1974.

We are a cooperative collectively owned and operated by its worker-members, several of whom are writers.

We are members of the Industrial Common Ownership Movement.

Our policy is to encourage writers to assume greater control over the production of their own books; and teachers, booksellers and readers generally to engage in a more active relationship with publisher and writer.

We attempt to keep our overheads as low as possible so as to keep our book prices down, and thereby benefiting readers.

We welcome response which will tell us what readers wish to read.

If you would like to be put on our mailing list and receive regular information about our books, please write to:

Writers and Readers Publishing Cooperative,
9-19 Rupert Street,
London W1V 7FS.